S0-CYF-693

CLASSIC

MYSTERIES II

A Collection of Mind-bending Masterpieces

Compiled by Glen & Karen Bledsoe

ROXBURY PARK

LOWELL HOUSE JUVENILE

LOS ANGELES

NTC/Contemporary Publishing Group

Published by Lowell House
A division of NTC/Contemporary Publishing Group, Inc.
4255 West Touhy Avenue, Lincolnwood (Chicago), Illinois 60646-1975 U.S.A.

Lowell House books can be purchased at special discounts when ordered in bulk
for premiums and special sales. Contact Department CS at the following address:
NTC/Contemporary Publishing Group
4255 West Touhy Avenue
Lincolnwood, IL 60646-1975
1-800-323-4900

ISBN: 0-7373-0273-9
Library of Congress Catalog Card Number: 99-71488

Roxbury Park is a division of NTC/Contemporary Publishing Group, Inc.

Managing Director and Publisher: Jack Artenstein
Editor in Chief, Roxbury Park Books: Michael Artenstein
Director of Publishing Services: Rena Copperman
Editorial Assistant: Nicole Monastirsky
Interior Artwork: Barbara Kiwak
Interior Typesetting: Andrea Reider

Printed and bound in the United States of America
99 00 01 DHD 10 9 8 7 6 5 4 3 2 1

CONTENTS

CLASSIC MYSTERIES

Introduction

Whodunits, detective stories—call them what you like, mysteries are one of the most popular story-telling forms of all time. They may be so short as to take only a minute to read, or they may run the length of a novel. Whatever the duration, there's no doubt this exciting, nail-biting genre will be around for years to come.

Each country develops its own style of mystery. In America, the hard-boiled, tough-guy detective was born in the pages of pulp magazines of the 1930s. In England, detectives are usually created with a gentler nature than their American counterparts—gentler but wiser. And who could be gentler and wiser than a Catholic priest? Father Brown is G. K. Chesterton's memorable contribution to the world of literary detectives. In "The Absence of Mr. Glass," we see this priestly sleuth poke a little fun at his fellow English detectives.

Father Brown is a simple name for a simple priest who solves not so simple mysteries. A name we *never* learn is that of the main character of Baroness Orczy's "Old Man in the Corner" stories. That we do not discover this detective's name only enhances the story, giving it a stranger, more mysterious quality than if we knew everything about the nameless, grotesque scarecrow of an "Old Man."

Few writers can claim to have done more to popularize the mystery story than Sir Arthur Conan Doyle. His character, Sherlock Holmes, has become *the* symbol representing detective fiction, but Holmes, the world's first consulting detective, is not the limit of Doyle's detective fiction. In "The Beetle Hunter" the protagonist isn't even a detective, merely an innocent participant.

Curiously enough, the central character in a mystery need not be on the side of the law. The French writer Maurice Leblanc focuses our attention not on the mastermind who solves the crimes, but on the mastermind who commits them: Arsène Lupin, gentleman burglar. In "The Arrest of Arsène Lupin," the reader receives the most pleasurable of all experiences of reading a mystery: the unexpected twist at the end.

Those unexpected twists, the "elementary" deductions, the bold and swift plans, and sometimes just the momentary escape from the real world are what we crave when we read mysteries. Turn the page and try your hand at solving these puzzles before the author beats you to the solution.

THE ABSENCE OF MR. GLASS
FROM *THE WISDOM OF FATHER BROWN*
G. K. Chesterton

Gilbert Keith Chesterton, born in England, began his writing career while studying art. Though he labeled himself a mere "rollicking journalist," he was a gifted writer whose talents extended to poetry, essays, novels, biographies, literary criticisms, humor, and mystery stories. Chesterton was outgoing, outspoken, strongly opinionated, and possessed the verbal talent to defend his ideas eloquently. His best known fictional character, however, is Father Brown, a quiet and simple priest who solves mysteries less by the deduction of observed evidence than by his knowledge of human nature. Though some of the Father Brown plots may border on the unlikely, they are meant to illustrate moral truths.

Chesterton was bitterly opposed to the Boer War in South Africa (1899 –1902) in which British troops clashed with the descendants of Dutch settlers. Sir Arthur Conan Doyle, author of another tale in this book and the creator of Sherlock Holmes, fought in the Boer War and his writings about the war earned him a knighthood. Perhaps this is why, in the following tale, we see Chesterton is poking fun at the type of detective exemplified by Sherlock Holmes.

The consulting rooms of Dr. Orion Hood, the eminent criminologist and specialist in certain moral disorders, lay along the seafront at Scarborough, in a series of very large and well-lighted french windows, which showed the North Sea like one endless outer wall of blue-green marble. In such a place the sea had something of the monotony of a blue-green dado: for the chambers themselves were ruled throughout by a terrible tidiness not unlike the terrible tidiness of the sea. It must not be supposed that Dr. Hood's apartments excluded luxury, or even poetry. These things were there, in their place; but one felt that they were never allowed out of their place. Luxury was there: There stood upon a special table eight or ten boxes of the best cigars; but they were built upon a plan so that the strongest were always nearest the wall and the mildest nearest the window. A tantalus containing three kinds of spirit, all of a liqueur excellence, stood always on this table of luxury; but the fanciful have asserted that the whisky, brandy, and rum seemed always to stand at the same level. Poetry was there: The left-hand corner of the room was lined with as complete a set of English classics as the right hand could show of English and foreign physiologists. But if one took a volume of Chaucer or Shelley from that rank, its absence irritated the mind like a gap in a man's front teeth. One could not say the books were never read; probably they were, but there was a sense of their being chained to their places, like the bibles in the old churches. Dr. Hood treated his private bookshelf as if it were a public library. And if this strict scientific intangibility steeped even the shelves laden with lyrics and ballads and the tables laden with drink and tobacco, it goes without saying that yet more of such heathen holiness protected the other shelves that held the specialist's library, and the other tables that sustained the frail and even fairylike instruments of chemistry or mechanics.

Dr. Hood paced the length of his string of apartments, bounded—as the boys' geographies say—on the east by the North Sea and on the west by the serried ranks of his sociological and criminologist library. He was clad in an artist's velvet, but with none of an artist's negligence; his hair was heavily shot with gray, but growing thick and healthy; his face was lean, but sanguine and expectant. Everything about him and his room indicated something at once rigid and restless, like that great northern sea by which (on pure principles of hygiene) he had built his home.

Fate, being in a funny mood, pushed the door open and introduced into those long, strict, sea-flanked apartments one who was perhaps the most startling opposite of them and their master. In answer to a curt but civil summons, the door opened inward and there shambled into the room a shapeless little figure, which seemed to find its own hat and umbrella as unmanageable as a mass of luggage. The umbrella was a black and prosaic bundle long past repair; the hat was a broad-curved black hat, clerical but not common in England; the man was the very embodiment of all that is homely and helpless.

The doctor regarded the newcomer with a restrained astonishment, not unlike that he would have shown if some huge but obviously harmless seabeast had crawled into his room. The newcomer regarded the doctor with that beaming but breathless geniality which characterizes a corpulent charwoman who has just managed to stuff herself into an omnibus. It is a rich confusion of social self-congratulation and bodily disarray. His hat tumbled to the carpet, his heavy umbrella slipped between his knees with a thud; he reached after the one and ducked after the other, but with an unimpaired smile on his round face spoke simultaneously as follows:

"My name is Brown. Pray excuse me. I've come about that business of the MacNabs. I have heard, you often help people out of such troubles. Pray excuse me if I am wrong."

By this time he had sprawlingly recovered the hat, and made an odd little bobbing bow over it, as if setting everything quite right.

"I hardly understand you," replied the scientist, with a cold intensity of manner. "I fear you have mistaken the chambers. I am Dr. Hood, and my work is almost entirely literary and educational. It is true that I have sometimes been consulted by the police in cases of peculiar difficulty and importance, but—"

"Oh, this is of the greatest importance," broke in the little man called Brown. "Why, her mother won't let them get engaged." And he leaned back in his chair in radiant rationality.

The brows of Dr. Hood were drawn down darkly, but the eyes under them were bright with something that might be anger or might be amusement. "And still," he said, "I do not quite understand."

"You see, they want to get married," said the man with the clerical hat. "Maggie MacNab and young Todhunter want to get married. Now, what can be more important than that?"

The great Orion Hood's scientific triumphs had deprived him of many things—some said of his health, others of his God; but they had not wholly despoiled him of his sense of the absurd. At the last plea of the ingenuous priest a chuckle broke out of him from inside, and he threw himself into an armchair in an ironical attitude of the consulting physician.

"Mr. Brown," he said gravely, "it is quite 14 1/2 years since I was personally asked to test a personal problem: then it was the case of an attempt to poison the French president at a Lord Mayor's banquet. It is now, I understand, a question of whether some friend of yours called Maggie is a suitable fiancée for some friend of hers called Todhunter. Well, Mr. Brown, I am a sportsman. I will take it on. I will give the MacNab family my best advice, as good as I gave the French Republic and the king of England—no, better: 14 years better. I have nothing else to do this afternoon. Tell me your story."

The little clergyman called Brown thanked him with unquestionable warmth, but still with a queer kind of simplicity. It was rather as if he were thanking a stranger in a smoking room for some trouble in passing the matches, than as if he were (as he was) practically thanking the curator of Kew Gardens for coming with him into a field to find a four-leaved clover. With scarcely a semicolon after his hearty thanks, the little man began his recital:

"I told you my name was Brown; well, that's the fact, and I'm the priest of the little Catholic church I dare say you've seen beyond those straggly streets, where the town ends toward the north. In the last and straggliest of those streets which runs along the sea like a seawall there is a very honest but rather sharp-tempered member of my flock, a widow called MacNab. She has one daughter, and she lets lodgings, and between her and the daughter, and between her and the lodgers—well, I dare say there is a great deal to be said on both sides. At present she has only one lodger, the young man called Todhunter; but he has given more trouble than all the rest, for he wants to marry the young woman of the house."

"And the young woman of the house," asked Dr. Hood, with huge and silent amusement, "what does she want?"

"Why, she wants to marry him," cried Father Brown, sitting up eagerly. "That is just the awful complication."

"It is indeed a hideous enigma," said Dr. Hood.

"This young James Todhunter," continued the cleric, "is a very decent man so far as I know; but then nobody knows very much. He is a bright, brownish little fellow, agile like a monkey, clean-shaven like an actor, and obliging like a born courtier. He seems to have quite a pocketful of money, but nobody knows what his trade is. Mrs. MacNab, therefore (being of a pessimistic turn), is quite sure it is something dreadful, and probably connected with dynamite. The dynamite must be of a shy and noiseless sort, for the poor fellow only shuts himself up for several hours of the day and studies something behind a locked door. He declares his privacy is temporary and justified, and promises to explain before the wedding. That is all that anyone knows for certain, but Mrs. MacNab will tell you a great deal more than even she is certain of. You know how the tales grow like grass on such a patch of ignorance as that. There are tales of two voices heard talking in the room; though, when the door is opened, Todhunter is always found alone. There are tales of a mysterious tall man in a silk hat, who once came out of the seamists and apparently out of the sea, stepping softly across the sandy fields and through the small back garden at twilight, till he was heard talking to the lodger at his open window. The colloquy seemed to end in a quarrel. Todhunter dashed down his window with violence, and the man in the high hat melted into the seafog again. This story is told by the family with the fiercest mystification; but I really think Mrs. MacNab prefers her own original tale: that the other man (or whatever it is) crawls out every night from the big box in the corner, which is kept locked all day. You see, therefore, how this sealed door of Todhunter's is treated as the gate of all the fancies and monstrosities of the 'Thousand and One Nights'. And yet there is the little fellow in his respectable black jacket, as punctual and innocent as a parlor clock. He pays his rent to the tick; he is practically a teetotaler; he is tirelessly kind with the younger children, and can keep them amused for a day on end; and, last and most urgent of all, he has made himself equally popular with the eldest daughter, who is ready to go to church with him tomorrow."

A man warmly concerned with any large theories has always a relish for applying them to any triviality. The great specialist having condescended to the priest's simplicity, condescended expansively. He settled himself with comfort in his armchair and began to talk in the tone of a somewhat absent-minded lecturer:

"Even in a minute instance, it is best to look first to the main tendencies of Nature. A particular flower may not be dead in early winter, but the flowers are dying; a particular pebble may never be wetted with the tide, but the tide is coming in. To the scientific eye all human history is a series of collective movements, destructions or migrations, like the massacre of flies in winter or the return of birds in spring. Now the root fact in all history is Race. Race produces religion; Race produces legal and ethical wars. There is no stronger case than that of the wild, unworldly and perishing stock which we commonly call the Celts, of whom your friends the MacNabs are specimens. Small, swarthy, and of this dreamy and drifting blood, they accept easily the superstitious explanation of any incidents, just as they still accept (you will excuse me for saying) that superstitious explanation of all incidents which you and your Church represent. It is not remarkable that such people, with the sea moaning behind them and the Church (excuse me again) droning in front of them, should put fantastic features into what are probably plain events. You, with your small parochial responsibilities, see only this particular Mrs. MacNab, terrified with this particular tale of two voices and a tall man out of the sea. But the man with the scientific imagination sees, as it were, the whole clans of MacNab scattered over the whole world, in its ultimate average as uniform as a tribe of birds. He sees thousands of Mrs. MacNabs, in thousands of houses, dropping their little drop of morbidity in the tea-cups of their friends; he sees—"

Before the scientist could conclude his sentence, another and more impatient summons sounded from without; someone with swishing skirts was marshaled hurriedly down the corridor, and the door opened on a young girl, decently dressed but disordered and red-hot with haste. She had sea-blown blond hair, and would have been entirely beautiful if her cheekbones had not been, in the Scotch manner, a little high in relief as well as in color. Her apology was almost as abrupt as a command.

"I'm sorry to interrupt you, sir," she said, "but I had to follow Father Brown at once; it's nothing less than life or death."

Father Brown began to get to his feet in some disorder. "Why, what has happened, Maggie?" he said.

"James has been murdered, for all I can make out," answered the girl, still breathing hard from her rush. "That man Glass has been with him again; I heard them talking through the door quite plain. Two separate voices: for James speaks low, with a burr, and the other voice was high and quavery."

"That man Glass?" repeated the priest in some perplexity.

"I know his name is Glass," answered the girl, in great impatience. "I heard it through the door. They were quarreling—about money, I think—for I heard James say again and again, 'That's right, Mr. Glass,' or 'No, Mr. Glass,' and then, 'Two or three, Mr. Glass.' But we're talking too much; you must come at once, and there may be time yet."

"But time for what?" asked Dr. Hood, who had been studying the young lady with marked interest. "What is there about Mr. Glass and his money troubles that should impel such urgency?"

"I tried to break down the door and couldn't," answered the girl shortly, "Then I ran to the backyard, and managed to climb onto the windowsill that looks into the room. It was dim, and seemed to be empty, but I swear I saw James lying huddled up in a corner, as if he were drugged or strangled."

"This is very serious," said Father Brown, gathering his errant hat and umbrella and standing up; "in point of fact I was just putting your case before this gentleman, and his view—"

"Has been largely altered," said the scientist gravely. "I do not think this young lady is so Celtic as I had supposed. As I have nothing else to do, I will put on my hat and stroll down town with you."

In a few minutes all three were approaching the dreary tail of the MacNabs's street: the girl with the stern and breathless stride of the mountaineer, the criminologist with a lounging grace (which was not without a certain leopardlike swiftness), and the priest at an energetic trot entirely devoid of distinction. The aspect of this edge of the town was not entirely without justification for the doctor's hints about desolate moods and environments. The scattered houses stood farther and farther apart in a broken string along the seashore; the afternoon was closing with a premature and partly lurid twilight; the sea was of an inky purple and murmuring ominously. In the scrappy back garden of the MacNabs which ran down toward the sand, two black, barren-looking trees stood up like demon hands held up in astonishment, and as Mrs. MacNab ran down the street to meet them with lean hands similarly spread, and her fierce face in shadow, she was a little like a demon herself. The doctor and the priest made scant reply to her shrill reiterations of her daughter's story, with more disturbing details of her own, to the divided vows of vengeance against Mr. Glass for murdering, and against Mr. Todhunter for being murdered, or against the latter for having dared to want to marry her daughter, and for not having lived to do it. They passed through the narrow passage in the front of the house until they came to the lodger's door at the back, and there Dr. Hood, with the trick of an old detective, put his shoulder sharply to the panel and burst in the door.

It opened on a scene of silent catastrophe. No one seeing it, even for a flash, could doubt that the room had been the theater of some thrilling collision between two, or perhaps more, persons. Playing cards lay littered across the table or fluttered about the floor as if a game had been interrupted. Two wine glasses stood ready for wine on a side table, but a third lay smashed in a star of crystal upon the carpet. A few feet from it lay what looked like a long knife or short sword, straight, but with an ornamental and pictured handle, its dull blade just caught a gray glint from the dreary window behind, which showed the black trees against the leaden level of the sea. Toward the opposite corner of the room was rolled a gentleman's silk top hat, as if it had just been knocked off his head;

so much so, indeed, that one almost looked to see it still rolling. And in the corner behind it, thrown like a sack of potatoes, but corded like a railway trunk, lay Mr. James Todhunter, with a scarf across his mouth, and six or seven ropes knotted round his elbows and ankles. His brown eyes were alive and shifted alertly.

Dr. Orion Hood paused for one instant on the doormat and drank in the whole scene of voiceless violence. Then he stepped swiftly across the carpet, picked up the tall silk hat, and gravely put it upon the head of the yet pinioned Todhunter. It was so much too large for him that it almost slipped down onto his shoulders.

"Mr. Glass's hat," said the doctor, returning with it and peering into the inside with a pocket lens. "How to explain the absence of Mr. Glass and the presence of Mr. Glass's hat? For Mr. Glass is not a careless man with his clothes. That hat is of a stylish shape and systematically brushed and burnished, though not very new. An old dandy, I should think."

"But, good heavens!" called out Miss MacNab, "aren't you going to untie the man first?"

"I say 'old' with intention, though not with certainty" continued the expositor; "my reason for it might seem a little farfetched. The hair of human beings falls out in very varying degrees, but almost always falls out slightly, and with the lens I should see the tiny hairs in a hat recently worn. It has none, which leads me to guess that Mr. Glass is bald. Now when this is taken with the high-pitched and querulous voice which Miss MacNab described so vividly (patience, my dear lady, patience), when we take the hairless head together with the tone common in senile anger, I should think we may deduce some advance in years. Nevertheless, he was probably vigorous, and he was

almost certainly tall. I might rely in some degree on the story of his previous appearance at the window, as a tall man in a silk hat, but I think I have more exact indication. This wineglass has been smashed all over the place, but one of its splinters lies on the high bracket beside the mantelpiece. No such fragment could have fallen there if the vessel had been smashed in the hand of a comparatively short man like Mr. Todhunter."

"By the way," said Father Brown, "might it not be as well to untie Mr. Todhunter?"

"Our lesson from the drinking-vessels does not end here," proceeded the specialist. "I may say at once that it is possible that the man Glass was bald or nervous through dissipation rather than age. Mr. Todhunter, as has been remarked, is a quiet thrifty gentleman, essentially an abstainer. These cards and wine cups are no part of his normal habit; they have been produced for a particular companion. But, as it happens, we may go farther. Mr. Todhunter may or may not possess this wine service, but there is no appearance of his possessing any wine. What, then, were these vessels to contain? I would at once suggest some brandy or whisky, perhaps of a luxurious sort, from a flask in the pocket of Mr. Glass. We have thus something like a picture of the man, or at least of the type: tall, elderly, fashionable, but somewhat frayed, certainly fond of play and strong waters, perhaps rather too fond of them. Mr. Glass is a gentleman not unknown on the fringes of society."

"Look here," cried the young woman, "if you don't let me pass to untie him I'll run outside and scream for the police."

"I should not advise you, Miss MacNab," said Dr. Hood gravely, "to be in any hurry to fetch the police. Father Brown, I seriously ask you to compose your flock, for their sakes, not for mine. Well, we have seen something of the figure and quality of

Mr. Glass; what are the chief facts known of Mr. Todhunter? They are substantially three: that he is economical, that he is more or less wealthy, and that he has a secret. Now, surely it is obvious that there are the three chief marks of the kind of man who is blackmailed. And surely it is equally obvious that the faded finery, the profligate habits, and the shrill irritation of Mr. Glass are the unmistakable marks of the kind of man who blackmails him. We have the two typical figures of a tragedy of hush money: on the one hand, the respectable man with a mystery; on the other, the West End vulture with a scent for a mystery. These two men have met here today and have quarreled, using blows and a bare weapon."

"Are you going to take those ropes off?" asked the girl stubbornly.

Dr. Hood replaced the silk hat carefully on the side table, and went across to the captive. He studied him intently, even moving him a little and half turning him round by the shoulders, but he only answered:

"No; I think these ropes will do very well till your friends the police bring the handcuffs."

Father Brown, who had been looking dully at the carpet, lifted his round face and said: "What do you mean?"

The man of science had picked up the peculiar dagger sword from the carpet and was examining it intently as he answered:

"Because you find Mr. Todhunter tied up," he said, "you all jump to the conclusion that Mr. Glass had tied him up; and then, I suppose, escaped. There are four objections to this: First, why should a gentleman so dressy as our friend Glass leave his hat behind him, if he left of his own free will? Second," he continued, moving toward the window, "this is the only exit, and it is locked on the inside. Third, this blade here has a tiny touch of blood at the point, but there is no wound on Mr. Todhunter. Mr. Glass took that wound away with him, dead or alive. Add to all this primary probability. It is much more likely that the blackmailed person would try to kill his incubus, rather than that the blackmailer would try to kill the goose that lays his golden egg. There, I think, we have a pretty complete story."

"But the ropes?" inquired the priest, whose eyes had remained open with a rather vacant admiration.

"Ah, the ropes," said the expert with a singular intonation. "Miss MacNab very much wanted to know why I did not set Mr. Todhunter free from his ropes. Well, I will tell her. I did not do it because Mr. Todhunter can set himself free from them at any minute he chooses."

"What?" cried the audience on quite different notes of astonishment.

"I have looked at all the knots on Mr. Todhunter," reiterated Hood quietly. "I happen to know something about knots; they are quite a branch of criminal science. Every one of those knots he has made himself and could loosen himself; not one of them would have been made by an enemy really trying to pinion him. The whole of this affair of the ropes is a clever fake, to make us think him the victim of the struggle instead of the wretched Glass, whose corpse may be hidden in the garden or stuffed up the chimney."

There was a rather depressed silence; the room was darkening, the sea-blighted boughs of the garden trees looked leaner and blacker than ever, yet they seemed to have come nearer to the window. One could almost fancy they were sea-monsters like krakens or cuttlefish, writhing polyps who had crawled up from the sea to see the end of this tragedy, even as he, the villain and victim of it, the terrible man in the tall hat, had once crawled up from the sea. For the whole air was dense with the morbidity of blackmail, which is the most morbid of human things because it is a crime concealing a crime; a black plaster on a blacker wound.

The face of the little Catholic priest, which was commonly complacent and even comic, had suddenly become knotted with a curious frown. It was not the blank curiosity of his first innocence. It was rather that creative curiosity which comes when a man has the beginnings of an idea. "Say it again, please," he said in a simple, bothered manner; "do you mean that Todhunter can tie himself up all alone and untie himself all alone?"

"That is what I mean," said the doctor.

"Jerusalem!" shouted Brown suddenly, "I wonder if it could possibly be that!"

He scuttled across the room rather like a rabbit, and peered with quite a new impulsiveness into the partially covered face of the captive. Then he turned his own rather fatuous face to the company. "Yes, that's it!" he cried in a certain excitement. "Can't you see it in the man's face? Why, look at his eyes!"

Both the professor and the girl followed the direction of his glance. And though the broad black scarf completely masked the lower half of Todhunter's visage, they did grow conscious of something struggling and intense about the upper part of it.

"His eyes do look queer," cried the young woman, strongly moved. "You brutes; I believe it's hurting him!"

"Not that, I think," said Dr. Hood; "the eyes have certainly a singular expression. But I should interpret those transverse wrinkles as expressing rather such slight psychological abnormality—"

"Oh, bosh!" cried Father Brown: "can't you see he's laughing?"

"Laughing!" repeated the doctor, with a start; "but what on earth can he be laughing at?"

"Well," replied the Reverend Brown apologetically, "not to put too fine a point on it, I think he is laughing at you. And indeed, I'm a little inclined to laugh at myself, now I know about it."

"Now you know about what?" asked Hood, in some exasperation.

"Now I know," replied the priest, "the profession of Mr. Todhunter."

He shuffled about the room, looking at one object after another with what seemed to be a vacant stare, and then invariably bursting into an equally vacant laugh, a highly irritating process for those who had to watch it. He laughed very much over the hat, still more uproariously over the broken glass, but the blood on the sword point sent him into mortal convulsions of amusement. Then he turned to the fuming specialist.

"Dr. Hood," he cried enthusiastically, "you are a great poet! You have called an uncreated being out of the void. How much more godlike that is than if you had only ferreted out the mere facts! Indeed, the mere facts are rather commonplace and comic by comparison."

"I have no notion what you are talking about," said Dr. Hood rather haughtily; "my facts are all inevitable, though necessarily incomplete. A place may be permitted to intuition, perhaps (or poetry if you prefer the term), but only because the corresponding details cannot as yet be ascertained. In the absence of Mr. Glass—"

"That's it, that's it," said the little priest, nodding quite eagerly, "that's the first idea to get fixed; the absence of Mr. Glass. He is so extremely absent. I suppose," he added reflectively, "that there was never anybody so absent as Mr. Glass."

"Do you mean he is absent from the town?" demanded the doctor.

"I mean he is absent from everywhere," answered Father Brown; "he is absent from the nature of things, so to speak."

"Do you seriously mean," said the specialist with a smile, "that there is no such person?"

The priest made a sign of assent. "It does seem a pity," he said.

Orion Hood broke into a contemptuous laugh. "Well," he said, "before we go on to the hundred and one other evidences, let us take the first proof we found; the first fact we fell over when we fell into this room. If there is no Mr. Glass, whose hat is this?"

"It is Mr. Todhunter's," replied Father Brown.

"But it doesn't fit him," cried Hood impatiently. "He couldn't possibly wear it!"

Father Brown shook his head with ineffable mildness. "I never said he could wear it," he answered. "I said it was his hat. Or, if you insist on a shade of difference, a hat that is his."

"And what is the shade of difference?" asked the criminologist with a slight sneer.

"My good sir," cried the mild little man, with his first movement akin to impatience, "if you will walk down the street to the nearest hatter's shop, you will see that there is, in common speech, a difference between a man's hat and the hats that are his."

"But a hatter," protested Hood, "can get money out of his stock of new hats. What could Todhunter get out of this one old hat?"

"Rabbits," replied Father Brown promptly.

"What?" cried Dr. Hood.

"Rabbits, ribbons, sweetmeats, goldfish, rolls of colored paper," said the reverend gentleman with rapidity. "Didn't you see it all when you found out the faked ropes? It's just the same with the sword. Mr. Todhunter hasn't got a scratch on him, as you say; but he's got a scratch in him, if you follow me."

"Do you mean inside Mr. Todhunter's clothes?" inquired Mrs. MacNab sternly.

"I do not mean inside Mr. Todhunter's clothes," said Father Brown. "I mean inside Mr. Todhunter."

"Well, what in the name of Bedlam do you mean?"

"Mr. Todhunter," explained Father Brown placidly, "is learning to be a professional conjurer, as well as juggler, ventriloquist, and expert in the rope trick. The conjuring explains the hat. It is without traces of hair, not because it is worn by the prematurely bald Mr. Glass, but because it has never been worn by anybody. The juggling explains the three glasses, which Todhunter was teaching himself to throw up and catch in rotation. But, being only at the stage of practice, he smashed one glass against the ceiling. And the juggling also explains the sword, which it was Mr. Todhunter's professional pride and duty to swallow. But, again, being at the stage of practice, he very slightly grazed the inside of his throat with the weapon. Hence he has a wound inside him, which I am sure (from the

expression on his face) is not a serious one. He was also practicing the trick of a release from ropes, like the Davenport
brothers, and he was just about to free himself when we all
burst into the room. The cards, of course, are for card tricks,
and they are scattered on the floor because he had just been
practicing one of those dodges of sending them flying through
the air. He merely kept his trade secret, because he had to keep
his tricks secret, like any other conjurer. But the mere fact of
an idler in a top hat having once looked in at his back window,
and been driven away by him with great indignation, was
enough to set us all on a wrong track of romance, and make us
imagine his whole life overshadowed by the silk-hatted specter
of Mr. Glass."

"But what about the two voices?" asked Maggie, staring.

"Have you never heard a ventriloquist?" asked Father
Brown. "Don't you know they speak first in their natural
voice, and then answer themselves in just that shrill, squeaky,
unnatural voice that you heard?"

There was a long silence, and Dr. Hood regarded the little
man who had spoken with a dark and attentive smile. "You are
certainly a very ingenious person," he said; "it could not have
been done better in a book. But there is just one part of Mr.
Glass you have not succeeded in explaining away, and that is
his name. Miss MacNab distinctly heard him so addressed by
Mr. Todhunter."

The Rev. Mr. Brown broke into a rather childish giggle.
"Well, that," he said, "that's the silliest part of the whole silly
story. When our juggling friend here threw up the three
glasses in turn, he counted them aloud as he caught them,
and also commented aloud when he failed to catch them.

What he really said was: 'One, two and three—missed a glass one, two—missed a glass.' And so on."

There was a second of stillness in the room, and then everyone with one accord burst out laughing. As they did so the figure in the corner complacently uncoiled all the ropes and let them fall with a flourish. Then, advancing into the middle of the room with a bow, he produced from his pocket a big bill printed in blue and red, which announced that Zaladin, the world's greatest conjurer, contortionist, ventriloquist and human kangaroo would be ready with an entirely new series of tricks at the Empire Pavilion, Scarborough, on Monday next at eight o'clock precisely.

THE MYSTERIOUS DEATH ON THE UNDERGROUND RAILWAY

The Baroness Orczy

*The Baroness Orczy (pronounced "OR-see"), brilliant, witty, darkly
attractive, was a frequent guest of some of the highest courts in Europe.
She dressed as flamboyantly as the aristocratic characters in her most
famous novel,* The Scarlet Pimpernel *(1905): low-cut gowns,
sparkling jewels, fanciful hats with huge ostrich plumes. She was, in
fact, an aristocrat herself, the only child of a Hungarian baron. In
1867 her father's peasants, afraid of losing work to the newly-intro-
duced farm machinery, burned the crops and farm buildings. The family gave up the land and moved away. The baroness lived in Brussels,
Budapest, London, Paris, and Monte Carlo. She studied music in
Europe, art in Great Britain, and by 17 could speak fluently in three
different languages. She studied painting, but decided she did not possess a visual artist's "sacred fire" and turned to writing instead. In her
lifetime the baroness wrote sixty-eight works, all in English.*

*The following tale is one of Baroness Orczy's short works,
which takes place about the turn of the twentieth century. In it, she
uses a technique called "framing." The action of the story is told to an
astonished listener by a stranger in a tea shop. The incident in the tea
shop is the frame for the true tale. This is but one of a group of similar
tales known as* The Old Man in the Corner *series.*

It was all very well for Mr. Richard Frobisher (of the London Mail) to cut up rough about it. Polly did not altogether blame him.

She liked him all the better for that frank outburst of man-like ill-temper which, after all said and done, was only a very flattering form of masculine jealousy.

Moreover, Polly distinctly felt guilty about the whole thing. She had promised to meet Dickie—that is Mr. Richard Frobisher—at two o'clock sharp outside the Palace Theater, because she wanted to go to a Maud Allan matinee, and because he naturally wished to go with her.

But at two o'clock sharp she was still in Norfolk Street, Strand, inside an A.B.C. shop, sipping cold coffee opposite a grotesque old man who was fiddling with a bit of string.

How could she be expected to remember Maud Allan or the Palace Theater, or Dickie himself for a matter of that? The man in the corner had begun to talk of that mysterious death on the Underground Railway, and Polly had lost count of time, of place, and circumstance.

She had gone to lunch quite early, for she was looking forward to the matinee at the Palace.

The old scarecrow was sitting in his accustomed place when she came into the A.B.C. shop, but he had made no remark all the time that the young girl was munching her scone and butter. She was just busy thinking how rude he was not even to have said "Good morning," when an abrupt remark from him caused her to look up.

"Will you be good enough," he said suddenly, "to give me a description of the man who sat next to you just now, while you were having your cup of coffee and scone."

Involuntarily Polly turned her head toward the distant door, through which a man in a light overcoat was even now quickly passing. That man had certainly sat at the next table to hers, when she first sat down to her coffee and scone; he had finished his luncheon—whatever it was—a moment ago, had paid at the desk and gone out. The incident did not appear to Polly as being of the slightest consequence.

Therefore she did not reply to the rude old man, but shrugged her shoulders, and called to the waitress to bring her bill.

"Do you know if he was tall or short, dark or fair?" continued the man in the corner, seemingly not the least disconcerted by the young girl's indifference. "Can you tell me at all what he was like?"

"Of course I can," rejoined Polly impatiently, "but I don't see that my description of one of the customers of an A.B.C. shop can have the slightest importance."

He was silent for a minute, while his nervous fingers fumbled about in his capacious pockets in search of the inevitable piece of string. When he had found this necessary "adjunct to thought," he viewed the young girl again through his half-closed lids, and added maliciously:

"But supposing it were of paramount importance that you should give an accurate description of a man who sat next to you for half an hour today, how would you proceed?"

"I should say that he was of medium height—"

"Five foot eight, nine, or ten?" he interrupted quietly.

"How can one tell to an inch or two?" rejoined Polly crossly. "He was between colors."

"What's that?" he inquired blandly.

"Neither fair nor dark—his nose—"

"Well, what was his nose like? Will you sketch it?"

"I am not an artist. His nose was fairly straight—his eyes—"

"Were neither dark nor light—his hair had the same striking peculiarity—he was neither short nor tall—his nose was neither aquiline nor snub—" he recapitulated sarcastically.

"No," she retorted; "he was just ordinary looking."

"Would you know him again—say tomorrow, and among a number of other men who were 'neither tall nor short, dark nor fair, aquiline nor snub-nosed,' etc.?"

"I don't know—I might—he was certainly not striking enough to be specially remembered."

"Exactly," he said, while he leant forward excitedly, for all the world like a jack-in-the-box let loose. "Precisely; and you are a journalist—call yourself one, at least—and it should be part of your business to notice and describe people. I don't mean only the wonderful personage with the clear Saxon features, the fine blue eyes, the noble brow and classic face, but the ordinary person—the person who represents ninety out of every hundred of his own kind—the average Englishman, say, of the middle classes, who is neither very tall nor very short, who wears a moustache which is neither fair nor dark, but which masks his mouth, and a top hat which hides the shape of his head and brow, a man, in fact, who dresses like hundreds of his fellow creatures, moves like them, speaks like them, has no peculiarity.

"Try to describe him, to recognize him, say a week hence, among his other 89 doubles; worse still, to swear his life away, if he happened to be implicated in some crime, wherein your recognition of him would place the halter round his neck.

"Try that, I say, and having utterly failed you will more readily understand how one of the greatest scoundrels unhung is still at large, and why the mystery on the Underground Railway was never cleared up.

"I think it was the only time in my life that I was seriously tempted to give the police the benefit of my own views upon the matter. You see, though I admire the brute for his cleverness, I did not see that his being unpunished could possibly benefit anyone.

"In these days of tubes and motor traction of all kinds, the old-fashioned best, cheapest, and quickest route to City and West End is often deserted, and the good old Metropolitan Railway carriages cannot at any time be said to be over-crowded. Anyway, when that particular train steamed into Aldgate at about 4 P.M. on March 18th last, the first-class carriages were all but empty.

"The guard marched up and down the platform looking into all the carriages to see if anyone had left a halfpenny evening paper behind for him, and opening the door of one of the first-class compartments, he noticed a lady sitting in the further corner, with her head turned away toward the window, evidently oblivious of the fact that on this line Aldgate is the terminal station.

" 'Where are you for, lady?' " he said.

"The lady did not move, and the guard stepped into the carriage, thinking that perhaps the lady was asleep. He touched her arm lightly and looked into her face. In his own poetic language, he was 'struck all of a 'eap.' In the glassy eyes, the ashen color of the cheeks, the rigidity of the head, there was the unmistakable look of death.

"Hastily the guard, having carefully locked the carriage door, summoned a couple of porters, and sent one of them off to the police station, and the other in search of the stationmaster.

"Fortunately at this time of day the up platform is not very crowded, all the traffic tending westward in the afternoon. It was only when an inspector and two police constables, accompanied by a detective in plain clothes and a medical officer, appeared upon the scene, and stood round a first-class railway compartment, that a few idlers realized that something unusual had occurred, and crowded round, eager and curious.

"Thus it was that the later editions of the evening papers, under the sensational heading, 'Mysterious Suicide on the Underground Railway,' had already an account of the extraordinary event. The medical officer had very soon come to the decision that the guard had not been mistaken, and that life was indeed extinct.

"The lady was young, and must have been very pretty before the look of fright and horror had so terribly distorted her features. She was very elegantly dressed, and the more frivolous papers were able to give their feminine readers a detailed account of the unfortunate woman's gown, her shoes, hat and gloves.

"It appears that one of the latter, the one on the right hand, was partly off, leaving the thumb and wrist bare. That hand held a small satchel, which the police opened, with a view to the possible identification of the deceased, but which was found to contain only a little loose silver, some smelling salts, and a small empty bottle, which was handed over to the medical officer for purposes of analysis.

"It was the presence of that small bottle which had caused the report to circulate freely that the mysterious case on the Underground Railway was one of suicide. Certain it was that neither about the lady's person, nor in the appearance of the railway carriage, was there the slightest sign of struggle or even of resistance. Only the look in the poor woman's eyes spoke of sudden terror, of the rapid vision of an unexpected and violent death, which probably only lasted an infinitesimal fraction of a second, but which had left its indelible mark upon the face, otherwise so placid and so still.

"The body of the deceased was conveyed to the mortuary. So far, of course, not a soul had been able to identify her, or to throw the slightest light upon the mystery which hung around her death.

"Against that, quite a crowd of idlers—genuinely interested or not—obtained admission to view the body, on the pretext of having lost or mislaid a relative or a friend. At about 8.30 P.M. a young man, very well dressed, drove up to the station in a hansom, and sent in his card to the superintendent. It was Mr. Hazeldene, shipping agent, of 11, Crown Lane, E.C., and No. 19, Addison Row, Kensington.

"The young man looked in a pitiable state of mental distress; his hand clutched nervously a copy of the *St James's Gazette*, which contained the fatal news. He said very little to the superintendent except that a person who was very dear to him had not returned home that evening.

"He had not felt really anxious until half an hour ago, when suddenly he thought of looking at his paper. The description of the deceased lady, though vague, had terribly alarmed him. He had jumped into a hansom, and now begged permission to view the body, in order that his worst fears might be allayed.

"You know what followed, of course," continued the man in the corner, "the grief of the young man was truly pitiable. In the woman lying there in a public mortuary before him, Mr. Hazeldene had recognized his wife.

"I am waxing melodramatic," said the man in the corner, who looked up at Polly with a mild and gentle smile, while his nervous fingers vainly endeavored to add another knot on the scrappy bit of string with which he was continually playing, "and I fear that the whole story savors of the penny novelette, but you must admit, and no doubt you remember, that it was an intensely pathetic and truly dramatic moment.

"The unfortunate young husband of the deceased lady was not much worried with questions that night. As a matter of fact, he was not in a fit condition to make any coherent statement. It was at the coroner's inquest on the following day that certain facts came to light, which for the time being seemed to clear up the mystery surrounding Mrs. Hazeldene's death, only to plunge that same mystery, later on, into denser gloom than before.

"The first witness at the inquest was, of course, Mr. Hazeldene himself. I think everyone's sympathy went out to the young man as he stood before the coroner and tried to throw what light he could upon the mystery. He was well-dressed, as he had been the day before, but he looked terribly ill and worried, and no doubt the fact that he had not shaved gave his face a careworn and neglected air.

"It appears that he and the deceased had been married some six years or so, and that they had always been happy in their married life. They had no children. Mrs. Hazeldene seemed to enjoy the best of health till lately, when she had had a slight attack of influenza, in which Dr. Arthur Jones had attended her. The doctor was present at this moment, and would no doubt explain to the coroner and the jury whether he thought that Mrs. Hazeldene had the slightest tendency to heart disease, which might have had a sudden and fatal ending.

"The coroner was, of course, very considerate to the bereaved husband. He tried by circumlocution to get at the point he wanted, namely, Mrs. Hazeldene's mental condition lately. Mr. Hazeldene seemed loath to talk about this. No doubt he had been warned as to the existence of the small bottle found in his wife's satchel.

" 'It certainly did seem to me at times,' he at last reluctantly admitted, 'that my wife did not seem quite herself. She used to be very happy and bright, and lately I often saw her in the evening sitting, as if brooding over some matters, which evidently she did not care to communicate to me.'

"Still the coroner insisted, and suggested the small bottle.

" 'I know, I know,' replied the young man, with a short, heavy sigh. 'You mean—the question of suicide—I cannot understand it at all—it seems so sudden and so terrible—she certainly had seemed listless and troubled lately—but only at times—and yesterday morning, when I went to business, she appeared quite herself again, and I suggested that we should go to the opera in the evening. She was delighted, I know, and told me she would do some shopping, and pay a few calls in the afternoon.'

" 'Do you know at all where she intended to go when she got into the Underground Railway?'

" 'Well, not with certainty. You see, she may have meant to get out at Baker Street, and go down to Bond Street to do her shopping. Then, again, she sometimes goes to a shop in St. Paul's Churchyard, in which case she would take a ticket to Aldersgate Street; but I cannot say.'

" 'Now, Mr. Hazeldene,' said the coroner at last very kindly, 'will you try to tell me if there was anything in Mrs. Hazeldene's life which you know of, and which might in some measure explain the cause of the distressed state of mind, which you yourself had noticed? Did there exist any financial difficulty which might have preyed upon Mrs. Hazeldene's mind; was there any friend—to whose relationship with Mrs. Hazeldene—you—er—at any time took exception? In fact,' added the coroner, as if thankful that he had got over an unpleasant moment, 'can you give me the slightest indication which would tend to confirm the suspicion that the unfortunate lady, in a moment of mental anxiety or derangement, may have wished to take her own life?'

"There was silence in the court for a few moments. Mr. Hazeldene seemed to everyone there present to be laboring under some terrible moral doubt. He looked very pale and wretched, and twice attempted to speak before he at last said in scarcely audible tones:

" 'No; there were no financial difficulties of any sort. My wife had an independent fortune of her own—she had no extravagant tastes—'

" 'Nor any friend you at any time objected to?' insisted the coroner.

" 'Nor any friend, I—at any time objected to,' stammered the unfortunate young man, evidently speaking with an effort.

"I was present at the inquest," resumed the man in the corner, after he had drunk a glass of milk and ordered another, "and I can assure you that the most obtuse person there plainly realized that Mr. Hazeldene was telling a lie. It was pretty plain to the meanest intelligence that the unfortunate lady had not fallen into a state of morbid dejection for nothing, and that perhaps there existed a third person who could throw more light on her strange and sudden death than the unhappy, bereaved young widower.

"That the death was more mysterious even than it had at first appeared became very soon apparent. You read the case at the time, no doubt, and must remember the excitement in the public mind caused by the evidence of the two doctors. Dr. Arthur Jones, the lady's usual medical man, who had attended her in a last very slight illness, and who had seen her in a professional capacity fairly recently, declared most emphatically that Mrs. Hazeldene suffered from no organic complaint which could possibly have been the cause of sudden death. Moreover, he had assisted Mr. Andrew Thornton, the district medical officer, in making a post-mortem examination, and together they had come to the conclusion that death was due to the action of prussic acid, which had caused instantaneous failure of the heart, but how the drug had been administered neither he nor his colleague were at present able to state.

" 'Do I understand, then, Dr. Jones, that the deceased died, poisoned with prussic acid?'

" 'Such is my opinion,' replied the doctor.

" 'Did the bottle found in her satchel contain prussic acid?'

" 'It had contained some at one time, certainly.'

" 'In your opinion, then, the lady caused her own death by taking a dose of that drug?'

" 'Pardon me, I never suggested such a thing: the lady died poisoned by the drug, but how the drug was administered we cannot say. By injection of some sort, certainly. The drug certainly was not swallowed; there was not a vestige of it in the stomach.'

" 'Yes,' added the doctor in reply to another question from the coroner, 'death had probably followed the injection in this case almost immediately; say within a couple of minutes, or perhaps three. It was quite possible that the body would not have more than one quick and sudden convulsion, perhaps not that; death in such cases is absolutely sudden and crushing.'

"I don't think that at the time anyone in the room realized how important the doctor's statement was, a statement, which, by the way, was confirmed in all its details by the district medical officer, who had conducted the postmortem. Mrs. Hazeldene had died suddenly from an injection of prussic acid, administered no one knew how or when. She had been traveling in a first-class railway carriage in a busy time of the day. That young and elegant woman must have had singular nerve and coolness to go through the process of a self-inflicted injection of a deadly poison in the presence of perhaps two or three other persons.

"Mind you, when I say that no one there realized the importance of the doctor's statement at that moment, I am wrong; there were three persons, who fully understood at once the gravity of the situation, and the astounding development which the case was beginning to assume.

"Of course, I should have put myself out of the question," added the weird old man, with that inimitable self-conceit peculiar to himself. "I guessed then and there in a moment where the police were going wrong, and where they would go on going wrong until the mysterious death on the

Underground Railway had sunk into oblivion, together with the other cases which they mismanage from time to time.

"I said there were three persons who understood the gravity of the two doctors' statements—the other two were, firstly, the detective who had originally examined the railway carriage, a young man of energy and plenty of misguided intelligence, the other was Mr. Hazeldene.

"At this point the interesting element of the whole story was first introduced into the proceedings, and this was done through the humble channel of Emma Funnel, Mrs. Hazeldene's maid, who, as far as was known then, was the last person who had seen the unfortunate lady alive and had spoken to her.

" 'Mrs. Hazeldene lunched at home,' explained Emma, who was shy, and spoke almost in a whisper; 'she seemed well and cheerful. She went out at about half-past three, and told me she was going to Spence's, in St. Paul's Churchyard to try on her new tailor-made gown. Mrs. Hazeldene had meant to go there in the morning, but was prevented as Mr. Errington called.'

" 'Mr. Errington?' asked the coroner casually. 'Who is Mr. Errington?'

"But this Emma found difficult to explain. Mr. Errington was—Mr. Errington, that's all.

" 'Mr. Errington was a friend of the family. He lived in a flat in the Albert Mansions. He very often came to Addison Row, and generally stayed late.'

"Pressed still further with questions, Emma at last stated that latterly Mrs. Hazeldene had been to the theater several times with Mr. Errington, and that on those nights the master looked very gloomy, and was very cross.

"Recalled, the young widower was strangely reticent. He gave forth his answers very grudgingly, and the coroner was evidently absolutely satisfied with himself at the marvelous way in which, after a quarter of an hour of firm yet very kind questionings, he had elicited from the witness what information he wanted.

"Mr. Errington was a friend of his wife. He was a gentleman of means, and seemed to have a great deal of time at his command. He himself did not particularly care about Mr. Errington, but he certainly had never made any observations to his wife on the subject.

" 'But who is Mr. Errington?' repeated the coroner once more. 'What does he do? What is his business or profession?'

" 'He has no business or profession.'

" 'What is his occupation, then?'

" 'He has no special occupation. He has ample private means. But he has a great and very absorbing hobby.'

" 'What is that?'

" 'He spends all his time in chemical experiments, and is, I believe, as an amateur, a very distinguished toxicologist.'

"Did you ever see Mr. Errington, the gentleman so closely connected with the mysterious death on the Underground Railway?" asked the man in the corner as he placed one or two of his little snapshot photos before Miss Polly Burton.

"There he is, to the very life. Fairly good-looking, a pleasant face enough, but ordinary, absolutely ordinary.

"It was this absence of any peculiarity which very nearly, but not quite, placed the halter round Mr. Errington's neck.

"But I am going too fast, and you will lose the thread. The public, of course, never heard how it actually came about that

Mr. Errington, the wealthy bachelor of Albert Mansions, of the Grosvenor, and other young dandies' clubs, one fine day found himself before the magistrates at Bow Street, charged with being concerned in the death of Mary Beatrice Hazeldene, late of No. 19, Addison Row.

"I can assure you both press and public were literally flabbergasted. You see, Mr. Errington was a well-known and very popular member of a certain smart section of London society. He was a constant visitor at the opera, the race course, the park, and the Carlton, he had a great many friends, and there was consequently quite a large attendance at the police court that morning. What had happened was this:

"After the very scrappy bits of evidence which came to light at the inquest, two gentlemen bethought themselves that perhaps they had some duty to perform toward the state and the public generally. Accordingly they had come forward offering to throw what light they could upon the mysterious affair on the Underground Railway.

"The police naturally felt that their information, such as it was, came rather late in the day, but as it proved of paramount importance, and the two gentlemen, moreover, were of undoubtedly good position in the world, they were thankful for what they could get, and acted accordingly; they accordingly brought Mr. Errington up before the magistrate on a charge of murder.

"The accused looked pale and worried when I first caught sight of him in the court that day, which was not to be wondered at, considering the terrible position in which he found himself. He had been arrested at Marseilles, where he was preparing to start for Colombo.

"I don't think he realized how terrible his position was until later in the proceedings, when all the evidence relating to the arrest had been heard, and Emma Funnel had repeated her statement as to Mr. Errington's call at 19, Addison Row, in the morning, and Mrs. Hazeldene starting off for St. Paul's Churchyard at 3:30 in the afternoon. Mr. Hazeldene had nothing to add to the statements he had made at the coroner's inquest. He had last seen his wife alive on the morning of the fatal day. She had seemed very well and cheerful.

"I think everyone present understood that he was trying to say as little as possible that could in any way couple his deceased wife's name with that of the accused.

"And yet, from the servant's evidence, it undoubtedly leaked out that Mrs. Hazeldene, who was young, pretty, and evidently fond of admiration, had once or twice annoyed her husband by her somewhat open, yet perfectly innocent flirtation with Mr. Errington.

"I think everyone was most agreeably impressed by the widower's moderate and dignified attitude. You will see his photo there, among this bundle. That is just how he appeared in court. In deep black, of course, but without any sign of ostentation in his mourning. He had allowed his beard to grow lately, and wore it closely cut in a point.

"After his evidence, the sensation of the day occurred. A tall, dark-haired man, with the word *City* written metaphorically all over him, had kissed the book, and was waiting to tell the truth, and nothing but the truth.

"He gave his name as Andrew Campbell, head of the firm of Campbell & Co., brokers, of Throgmorton Street.

"In the afternoon of March 18th Mr. Campbell, traveling on the Underground Railway, had noticed a very pretty woman in the same carriage as himself. She had asked him if she was in the right train for Aldersgate. Mr. Campbell replied in the affirmative, and then buried himself in the Stock Exchange quotations of his evening paper.

"At Gower Street, a gentleman in a tweed suit and bowler hat got into the carriage, and took a seat opposite the lady. She seemed very much astonished at seeing him, but Mr. Campbell did not recollect the exact words she said.

"The two talked to one another a good deal, and certainly the lady appeared animated and cheerful. Witness took no notice of them; he was very much engrossed in some calculations, and finally got out at Farringdon Street. He noticed that the man in the tweed suit also got out close behind him, having shaken hands with the lady, and said in a pleasant way: 'Au revoir! Don't be late tonight.' Mr. Campbell did not hear the lady's reply, and soon lost sight of the man in the crowd.

"Everyone was on tenterhooks, and eagerly waiting for the palpitating moment when witness would describe and identify the man who last had seen and spoken to the unfortunate woman, within five minutes probably of her strange and unaccountable death.

"Personally I knew what was coming before the Scotch stockbroker spoke. I could have jotted down the graphic and lifelike description he would give of a probable murderer. It would have fitted equally well the man who sat and had luncheon at this table just now; it would certainly have described five out of every ten young Englishmen you know.

"The individual was of medium height, he wore a moustache which was not very fair nor yet very dark, his hair was between colors. He wore a bowler hat, and a tweed suit—and—and—that was all—Mr. Campbell might perhaps know him again, but then again, he might not— he was not paying much attention—the gentleman was sitting on the same side of the carriage as himself—and he had his hat on all the time. He himself was busy with his newspaper—yes—he might know him again—but he really could not say.

"Mr. Andrew Campbell's evidence was not worth very much, you will say. No, it was not in itself, and would not have justified any arrest were it not for the additional statements made by Mr. James Verner, manager of Messrs Rodney & Co., color printers.

"Mr. Verner is a personal friend of Mr. Andrew Campbell, and it appears that at Farringdon Street, where he was waiting for his train, he saw Mr. Campbell get out of a first class railway carriage. Mr. Verner spoke to him for a second, and then, just as the train was moving off, he stepped into the same compartment which had just been vacated by the stockbroker and the man in the tweed suit. He vaguely recollects a lady sitting in the opposite corner to his own, with her face turned away from him, apparently asleep, but he paid no special attention to her. He was like nearly all businessmen when they are traveling—engrossed in his paper. Presently a special quotation interested him; he wished to make a note of it, took out a pencil from his waistcoat pocket, and seeing a clean piece of pasteboard on the floor, he picked it up, and scribbled on it the memorandum, which he wished to keep. He then slipped the card into his pocketbook."

" 'It was only two or three days later,' added Mr. Verner in the midst of breathless silence, 'that I had occasion to refer to these same notes again.

" 'In the meanwhile the papers had been full of the mysterious death on the Underground Railway, and the names of those connected with it were pretty familiar to me. It was, therefore, with much astonishment that on looking at the pasteboard which I had casually picked up in the railway carriage I saw the name on it, Frank Errington.'

"There was no doubt that the sensation in court was almost unprecedented. Never since the days of the Fenchurch Street mystery, and the trial of Smethurst, had I seen so much excitement. Mind you, I was not excited—I knew by now every detail of that crime as if I had committed it myself. In fact, I could not have done it better, although I have been a student of crime for many years now. Many people there—his friends, mostly—believed that Errington was doomed. I think he thought so, too, for I could see that his face was terribly white, and he now and then passed his tongue over his lips, as if they were parched.

"You see he was in the awful dilemma—a perfectly natural one, by the way—of being absolutely incapable of proving an alibi. The crime—if crime there was—had been committed three weeks ago. A man about town like Mr. Frank Errington might remember that he spent certain hours of a special afternoon at his club, or in the park, but it is very doubtful in nine cases out of ten if he can find a friend who could positively swear as to having seen him there. No! No! Mr. Errington was in a tight corner, and he knew it. You see, there were—besides the evidence—two or three circumstances which did not improve matters for him. His hobby in the direction of toxi-cology, to begin with. The police had found in his room every description of poisonous substances, including prussic acid.

"Then, again, that journey to Marseilles, the start for Colombo, was, though perfectly innocent, a very unfortunate one. Mr. Errington had gone on an aimless voyage, but the pub-lic thought that he had fled, terrified at his own crime. Sir Arthur Inglewood, however, here again displayed his mar-velous skill on behalf of his client by the masterly way in which he literally turned all the witnesses for the crown inside out.

"Having first got Mr. Andrew Campbell to state positively that in the accused he certainly did not recognize the man in the tweed suit, the eminent lawyer, after 20 minutes' cross-examination, had so completely upset the stockbroker's equa-nimity that it is very likely he would not have recognized his own office-boy.

"But through all his flurry and all his annoyance Mr. Andrew Campbell remained very sure of one thing; namely, that the lady was alive and cheerful, and talking pleasantly with the man in the tweed suit up to the moment when the latter, having shaken hands with her, left her with a pleasant 'Au revoir! Don't be late tonight.' He had heard neither scream nor struggle, and in his opinion, if the individual in the tweed suit had administered a dose of poison to his companion, it must have been with her own knowledge and free will; and the lady in the train most emphatically neither looked nor spoke like a woman prepared for a sudden and violent death.

"Mr. James Verner, against that, swore equally positively that he had stood in full view of the carriage door from the moment that Mr. Campbell got out until he himself stepped

into the compartment, that there was no one else in that carriage between Farringdon Street and Aldgate, and that the
lady, to the best of his belief, had made no movement during
the whole of that journey.

"No; Frank Errington was not committed for trial on the
capital charge," said the man in the corner with one of his sardonic smiles, "thanks to the cleverness of Sir Arthur
Inglewood, his lawyer. He absolutely denied his identity with
the man in the tweed suit, and swore he had not seen Mrs.
Hazeldene since 11 A.M. on that fatal day. There was no proof
that he had; moreover, according to Mr. Campbell's opinion,
the man in the tweed suit was in all probability not the murderer. Common sense would not admit that a woman could
have a deadly poison injected into her without her knowledge,
while chatting pleasantly to her murderer.

"Mr. Errington lives abroad now. He is about to marry. I
don't think any of his real friends for a moment believed that
he committed the dastardly crime. The police think they know
better. They do know this much, that it could not have been
a case of suicide, that if the man who undoubtedly traveled
with Mrs. Hazeldene on that fatal afternoon had no crime
upon his conscience he would long ago have come forward and
thrown what light he could upon the mystery.

"As to who that man was, the police in their blindness
have not the faintest doubt. Under the unshakable belief that
Errington is guilty they have spent the last few months in
unceasing labor to try and find further and stronger proofs of
his guilt. But they won't find them, because there are none.
There are no positive proofs against the actual murderer, for
he was one of those clever blackguards who think of every-

thing, foresee every eventuality, who know human nature well and can foretell exactly what evidence will be brought against them, and act accordingly.

"This blackguard from the first kept the figure, the personality, of Frank Errington before his mind. Frank Errington was the dust which the scoundrel threw metaphorically in the eyes of the police, and you must admit that he succeeded in blinding them—to the extent even of making them entirely forget the one simple little sentence, overheard by Mr. Andrew Campbell, and which was, of course, the clue to the whole thing—the only slip the cunning rogue made—'Au revoir! Don't be late tonight.'

"Mrs. Hazeldene was going that night to the opera with her husband.

"You are astonished?" he added with a shrug of the shoulders, "you do not see the tragedy yet, as I have seen it before me all along. The frivolous young wife, the flirtation with the friend?—all a blind, all presence. I took the trouble which the police should have taken immediately, of finding out something about the finances of the Hazeldene ménage. Money is in nine cases out of ten the keynote to a crime.

"I found that the will of Mary Beatrice Hazeldene had been proved by the husband, her sole executor, the estate being sworn at £15,000. I found out, moreover, that Mr. Edward Sholto Hazeldene was a poor shipper's clerk when he married the daughter of a wealthy builder in Kensington—and then I made note of the fact that the disconsolate widower had allowed his beard to grow since the death of his wife.

"There's no doubt that he was a clever rogue," added the strange creature, leaning excitedly over the table, and peering into Polly's face. "Do you know how that deadly poison was injected into the poor woman's system? By the simplest of all means, one known to every scoundrel in southern Europe. A ring—yes! A ring, which has a tiny hollow needle capable of holding a sufficient quantity of prussic acid to have killed two persons instead of one. The man in the tweed suit shook hands with his fair companion—probably she hardly felt the prick, not sufficiently in any case to make her utter a scream. And, mind you, the scoundrel had every facility, through his friendship with Mr. Errington, of procuring what poison he required, not to mention his friend's visiting card. We cannot gauge how many months ago he began to try and copy Frank Errington in his style of dress, the cut of his moustache, his general appearance, making the change probably so gradual, that no one in his own entourage would notice it. He selected for his model a man his own height and build, with the same colored hair."

"But there was the terrible risk of being identified by his fellow-traveler in the Underground," suggested Polly.

"Yes, there certainly was that risk; he chose to take it, and he was wise. He reckoned that several days would in any case elapse before that person, who, by the way, was a businessman absorbed in his newspaper, would actually see him again. The great secret of successful crime is to study human nature," added the man in the corner, as he began looking for his hat and coat. "Edward Hazeldene knew it well."

"But the ring?"

"He may have bought that when he was on his honeymoon," he suggested with a grim chuckle; "the tragedy was not planned in a week, it may have taken years to mature.

But you will own that there goes a frightful scoundrel unhung. I have left you his photograph as he was a year ago, and as he is now. You will see he has shaved his beard again, but also his moustache. I fancy he is a friend now of Mr. Andrew Campbell."

He left Miss Polly Burton wondering, not knowing what to believe.

And that is why she missed her appointment with Mr. Richard Frobisher (of the *London Mail*) to go and see Maud Allan dance at the Palace Theater that afternoon.

THE BEETLE HUNTER
FROM *THE STRAND MAGAZINE*
Sir Arthur Conan Doyle

*Though Sir Arthur Conan Doyle is best known as the creator of
Sherlock Holmes, the Holmes adventures represent only a fraction of
his work. Doyle was a prolific writer whose genius shines most bril-
liantly in his short stories.*

*Doyle studied medicine in Edinburgh, Scotland, and went to
work as a medical assistant to a Dr. Reginald Ratcliffe Hoare in
Birmingham. Had he made a better living in medicine, the world might
never have known of his talents. Because his salary was so small, Doyle
tried writing stories for the many literary magazines of the day in order
to supplement his income. Doyle's first story "The Mystery of Sasassa
Valley," was published in 1879; his first book,* A Study in Scarlet,
was published in 1887, and introduced the world to Sherlock Holmes.

*But the Holmes stories were hardly Doyle's favorites of his own
works. He preferred his longer historical novels, such as* The White
Company *(1897), which took years to research and write. It is his
short stories and adventures, however, that modern readers treasure: the
Professor Challenger tales (such as* The Lost World *and* The Poison
Belt*), the Sherlock Holmes adventures, and tales such as the one presented here, the strange story of the beetle hunter.*

*Doyle briefly set aside his writing career to serve in the British
army in South Africa during the Boer War (1899 – 1902). His*

pamphlet, *The War in South Africa* (1902), earned him a knighthood the same year.

———————————

A curious experience? said the doctor. Yes, my friends, I have had one very curious experience. I never expect to have another, for it is against all doctrines of chances that two such events would befall any one man in a single lifetime. You may believe me or not, but the thing happened exactly as I tell it.

I had just become a medical man, but I had not started in practice, and I lived in rooms in Gower Street. The street has been renumbered since then, but it was in the only house which has a bow window, upon the left-hand side as you go down from the Metropolitan Station. A widow named Murchison kept the house at that time, and she had three medical students and one engineer as lodgers. I occupied the top room, which was the cheapest, but cheap as it was it was more than I could afford. My small resources were dwindling away, and every week it became more necessary that I should find something to do. Yet I was very unwilling to go into general practice, for my tastes were all in the direction of science, and especially of zoology, toward which I had always a strong leaning. I had almost given the fight up and resigned myself to being a medical drudge for life, when the turning point of my struggles came in a very extraordinary way.

One morning I had picked up the *Standard* and was glancing over its contents. There was a complete absence of news, and I was about to toss the paper down again, when my eyes were caught by an advertisement at the head of the personal column. It was worded in this way:

Wanted for one or more days the services of a
medical man. It is essential that he should be a
man of strong physique, of steady nerves, and of
a resolute nature. Must be an entomologist—
coleopterist preferred. Apply, in person, at 77B,
Brook Street. Application must be made before
12 P.M. today.

Now, I have already said that I was devoted to zoology. Of
all branches of zoology, the study of insects was the most attractive to me, and of all insects beetles were the species with which
I was most familiar. Butterfly collectors are numerous, but beetles are far more varied, and more accessible in these islands
than are butterflies. It was this fact which had attracted my
attention to them, and I had myself made a collection which
numbered some hundred varieties. As to the other requisites
of the advertisement, I knew that my nerves could be depended
upon, and I had won the weight-throwing competition at the
interhospital sports. Clearly, I was the very man for the vacancy. Within five minutes of my having read the advertisement I
was in a cab and on my way to Brook Street.

As I drove, I kept turning the matter over in my head and
trying to make a guess as to what sort of employment it could
be which needed such curious qualifications. A strong
physique, a resolute nature, a medical training, and a knowledge of beetles—what connection could there be between
these various requisites? And then there was the disheartening
fact that the situation was not a permanent one, but ter-
minable from day to day, according to the terms of the advertisement. The more I pondered over it, the more unintelligible
did it become; but at the end of my meditations I always came

back to the ground fact that, come what might, I had nothing to lose, that I was completely at the end of my resources, and that I was ready for any adventure, however desperate, which would put a few honest sovereigns into my pocket. The man fears to fail who has to pay for his failure, but there was no penalty which fortune could exact from me. I was like the gambler with empty pockets, who is still allowed to try his luck with the others.

No. 77B, Brook Street, was one of those dingy and yet imposing houses, dun-colored and flat-faced, with the intensely respectable and solid air which marks the Georgian builder. As I alighted from the cab, a young man came out of the door and walked swiftly down the street. In passing me, I noticed that he cast an inquisitive and somewhat malevolent glance at me, and I took the incident as a good omen, for his appearance was that of a rejected candidate, and if he resented my application it meant that the vacancy was not yet filled up. Full of hope, I ascended the broad steps and rapped with the heavy knocker.

A footman in powder and livery opened the door. Clearly I was in touch with the people of wealth and fashion.

"Yes, sir?" said the footman.

"I came in answer to—"

"Quite so, sir," said the footman. "Lord Linchmere will see you at once in the library."

Lord Linchmere! I had vaguely heard the name, but could not for the instant recall anything about him. Following the footman, I was shown into a large, book-lined room in which there was seated behind a writing desk a small man with a pleasant, clean-shaven, mobile face, and long hair shot with gray, brushed back from his forehead. He looked me up and down with a very shrewd, penetrating glance, holding the card which the footman had given him in his right hand. Then he smiled pleasantly, and I felt that externally at any rate I possessed the qualifications which he desired.

"You have come in answer to my advertisement, Dr. Hamilton?" he asked.

"Yes, sir."

"Do you fulfill the conditions which are there laid down?"

"I believe that I do."

"You are a powerful man, or so I should judge from your appearance."

"I think that I am fairly strong."

"And resolute?"

"I believe so."

"Have you ever known what it was to be exposed to imminent danger?"

"No, I don't know that I ever have."

"But you think you would be prompt and cool at such a time?"

"I hope so."

"Well, I believe that you would. I have the more confidence in you because you do not pretend to be certain as to what you would do in a position that was new to you. My impression is that, so far as personal qualities go, you are the very man of whom I am in search. That being settled, we may pass on to the next point."

"Which is?"

"To talk to me about beetles."

I looked across to see if he was joking, but, on the contrary, he was leaning eagerly forward across his desk, and there was an expression of something like anxiety in his eyes.

"I am afraid that you do not know about beetles," he cried.

"On the contrary, sir, it is the one scientific subject about which I feel that I really do know something."

"I am overjoyed to hear it. Please talk to me about beetles."

I talked. I do not profess to have said anything original upon the subject, but I gave a short sketch of the characteristics of the beetle, and ran over the more common species, with some allusions to the specimens in my own little collection and to the article upon "Burying Beetles" which I had contributed to the *Journal of Entomological Science.*

"What! Not a collector?" cried Lord Linchmere. "You don't mean that you are yourself a collector?" His eyes danced with pleasure at the thought. "You are certainly the very man in London for my purpose. I thought that among five millions of people there must be such a man, but the difficulty is to lay one's hands upon him. I have been extraordinarily fortunate in finding you."

He rang a gong upon the table, and the footman entered.

"Ask Lady Rossiter to have the goodness to step this way," said his lordship, and a few moments later the lady was ushered into the room. She was a small, middle-aged woman, very like Lord Linchmere in appearance, with the same quick, alert features and gray-black hair. The expression of anxiety, however, which I had observed upon his face was very much more marked upon hers. Some great grief seemed to have cast its shadow over her features. As Lord Linchmere presented me she turned her face full upon me, and I was shocked to observe a half-healed scar extending for two inches over her right eyebrow. It was partly concealed by plaster, but nonetheless I could see that it had been a serious wound and not long inflicted.

"Dr. Hamilton is the very man for our purpose, Evelyn," said Lord Linchmere. "He is actually a collector of beetles, and he has written articles upon the subject."

"Really!" said Lady Rossiter. "Then you must have heard of my husband. Everyone who knows anything about beetles must have heard of Sir Thomas Rossiter."

For the first time a thin little ray of light began to break into the obscure business. Here, at last, was a connection between these people and beetles. Sir Thomas Rossiter—he was the greatest authority upon the subject in the world. He had made it his lifelong study, and had written a most exhaustive work upon it. I hastened to assure her that I had read and appreciated it.

"Have you met my husband?" she asked.

"No, I have not."

"But you shall," said Lord Linchmere, with decision.

The lady was standing beside the desk, and she put her hand upon his shoulder. It was obvious to me as I saw their faces together that they were brother and sister.

"Are you really prepared for this, Charles? It is noble of you, but you fill me with fears." Her voice quavered with apprehension, and he appeared to me to be equally moved, though he was making strong efforts to conceal his agitation.

"Yes, yes, dear; it is all settled, it is all decided; in fact, there is no other possible way, that I can see."

"There is one obvious way."

"No, no, Evelyn, I shall never abandon you—never. It will come right—depend upon it; it will come right, and surely it looks like the interference of Providence that so perfect an instrument should be put into our hands."

My position was embarrassing, for I felt that for the instant they had forgotten my presence. But Lord Linchmere came back suddenly to me and to my engagement.

"The business for which I want you, Dr. Hamilton, is that you should put yourself absolutely at my disposal. I wish you to come for a short journey with me, to remain always at my side, and to promise to do without question whatever I may ask you, however unreasonable it may appear to you to be."

"That is a good deal to ask," said I.

"Unfortunately I cannot put it more plainly, for I do not myself know what turn matters may take. You may be sure, however, that you will not be asked to do anything which your conscience does not approve; and I promise you that, when all is over, you will be proud to have been concerned in so good a work."

"If it ends happily," said the lady.

"Exactly; if it ends happily," his lordship repeated.

"And terms?" I asked.

"Twenty pounds a day."

I was amazed at the sum, and must have showed my surprise upon my features.

"It is a rare combination of qualities, as must have struck you when you first read the advertisement," said Lord Linchmere; "such varied gifts may well command a high return, and I do not conceal from you that your duties might be arduous or even dangerous. Besides, it is possible that one or two days may bring the matter to an end."

"Please God!" sighed his sister.

"So now, Dr. Hamilton, may I rely upon your aid?"

"Most undoubtedly," said I. "You have only to tell me what my duties are."

"Your first duty will be to return to your home. You will pack up whatever you may need for a short visit to the country. We start together from Paddington Station at 3:40 this afternoon."

"Do we go far?"

"As far as Pangbourne. Meet me at the bookstall at 3:30. I shall have the tickets. Goodbye, Dr. Hamilton! And, by the way, there are two things which I should be very glad if you would bring with you, in case you have them. One is your case for collecting beetles, and the other is a stick, and the thicker and heavier the better."

You may imagine that I had plenty to think of from the time that I left Brook Street until I set out to meet Lord Linchmere at Paddington. The whole fantastic business kept arranging and rearranging itself in kaleidoscopic forms inside my brain, until I had thought out a dozen explanations, each of them more grotesquely improbable than the last. And yet I felt that the truth must be something grotesquely improbable also. At last I gave up all attempts at finding a solution, and contented myself with exactly carrying out the instructions which I had received. With a hand valise, specimen case, and a loaded cane, I was waiting at the Paddington bookstall when Lord Linchmere arrived. He was an even smaller man than I had thought—frail and peaky, with a manner which was more nervous than it had been in the morning. He wore a long, thick traveling ulster, and I observed that he carried a heavy blackthorn cudgel in his hand.

"I have the tickets," said he, leading the way up the platform.

"This is our train. I have engaged a carriage, for I am particularly anxious to impress one or two things upon you while we travel down."

And yet all that he had to impress upon me might have been said in a sentence, for it was that I was to remember that I was there as a protection to himself, and that I was not on any consideration to leave him for an instant. This he repeated again and again as our journey drew to a close, with an insistence which showed that his nerves were thoroughly shaken.

"Yes," he said at last, in answer to my looks rather than to my words, "I am nervous, Dr. Hamilton. I have always been a timid man, and my timidity depends upon my frail physical health. But my soul is firm, and I can bring myself up to face a danger which a less nervous man might shrink from. What I am doing now is done from no compulsion, but entirely from a sense of duty, and yet it is, beyond doubt, a desperate risk. If things should go wrong, I will have some claims to the title of martyr."

This eternal reading of riddles was too much for me. I felt that I must put a term to it.

"I think it would very much better, sir, if you were to trust me entirely," said I. "It is impossible for me to act effectively, when I do not know what are the objects which we have in view, or even where we are going."

"Oh, as to where we are going, there need be no mystery about that," said he; "we are going to Delamere Court, the residence of Sir Thomas Rossiter, with whose work you are so conversant. As to the exact object of our visit, I do not know that at this stage of the proceedings anything would be gained, Dr. Hamilton, by taking you into my complete confidence. I may tell you that we are acting—I say 'we,' because my sister, Lady Rossiter, takes the same view as myself—with the one object of preventing anything in the nature of a family scandal. That being so, you can understand that I am loath to give any explanations which are not absolutely necessary. It would be a different matter, Dr. Hamilton, if I were asking your advice. As matters stand, it is only your active help which I need, and I will indicate to you from time to time how you can best give it."

There was nothing more to be said, and a poor man can put up with a good deal for 20 pounds a day, but I felt nonetheless that Lord Linchmere was acting rather scurvily toward me. He wished to convert me into a passive tool, like the blackthorn in his hand. With his sensitive disposition I could imagine, however, that scandal would be abhorrent to him, and I realized that he would not take me into his confidence until no other course was open to him. I must trust to my own eyes and ears to solve the mystery, but I had every confidence that I should not trust to them in vain.

Delamere Court lies a good five miles from Pangbourne Station, and we drove for that distance in an open fly. Lord Linchmere sat in deep thought during the time, and he never opened his mouth until we were close to our destination. When he did speak it was to give me a piece of information which surprised me.

"Perhaps you are not aware," said he, "that I am a medical man like yourself?"

"No, sir, I did not know it."

"Yes, I qualified in my younger days, when there were several lives between me and the peerage. I have not had occasion to practice, but I have found it a useful education, all the same. I never regretted the years which I devoted to medical study. These are the gates of Delamere Court."

We had come to two high pillars crowned with heraldic monsters which flanked the opening of a winding avenue. Over the laurel bushes and rhododendrons, I could see a long, many-gabled mansion, girdled with ivy, and toned to the warm, cheery, mellow glow of old brickwork. My eyes were still fixed in admiration upon this delightful house when my companion plucked nervously at my sleeve.

"Here's Sir Thomas," he whispered. "Please talk beetle all you can."

A tall, thin figure, curiously angular and bony, had emerged through a gap in the hedge of laurels. In his hand he held a spud, and he wore gauntleted gardener's gloves. A broad-brimmed, gray hat cast his face into shadow, but it struck me as exceedingly austere, with an ill-nourished beard and harsh, irregular features. The fly pulled up and Lord Linchmere sprang out.

"My dear Thomas, how are you?" said he, heartily.

But the heartiness was by no means reciprocal. The owner of the grounds glared at me over his brother-in-law's shoulder, and I caught broken scraps of sentences—"well-known wishes . . . hatred of strangers . . . unjustifiable intrusion . . . perfectly inexcusable." Then there was a muttered explanation, and the two of them came over together to the side of the fly.

"Let me present you to Sir Thomas Rossiter, Dr. Hamilton," said Lord Linchmere. "You will find that you have a strong community of tastes."

I bowed. Sir Thomas stood very stiffly, looking at me severely from under the broad brim of his hat.

"Lord Linchmere tells me that you know something about beetles," said he. "What do you know about beetles?"

"I know what I have learned from your work upon the coleoptera, Sir Thomas," I answered.

"Give me the names of the better-known species of the British scarabaei," said he.

I had not expected an examination, but fortunately I was ready for one. My answers seemed to please him, for his stern features relaxed.

"You appear to have read my book with some profit, sir," said he. "It is a rare thing for me to meet anyone who takes an intelligent interest in such matters. People can find time for such trivialities as sport or society, and yet the beetles are overlooked. I can assure you that the greater part of the idiots in this part of the country are unaware that I have ever written a book at all—I, the first man who ever described the true function of the elytra. I am glad to see you, sir, and I have no doubt that I can show you some specimens which will interest you." He stepped into the fly and drove up with us to the house, expounding to me as we went some recent researches which he had made into the anatomy of the ladybird.

I have said that Sir Thomas Rossiter wore a large hat drawn down over his brows. As he entered the hall he uncovered himself, and I was at once aware of a singular characteristic which the hat had concealed. His forehead, which was naturally high, and higher still on account of receding hair, was in a continual state of movement. Some nervous weakness kept the muscles in a constant spasm, which sometimes produced a mere twitching and sometimes a curious rotary movement unlike anything which I had ever seen before. It was strikingly visible as he turned toward us after entering the study, and seemed the more singular from the contrast with the hard, steady, gray eyes which looked out from underneath those palpitating brows.

"I am sorry," said he, "that Lady Rossiter is not here to help me to welcome you. By the way, Charles, did Evelyn say anything about the date of her return?"

"She wished to stay in town for a few more days," said Lord Linchmere. "You know how ladies' social duties accumulate if they have been for some time in the country. My sister has many old friends in London at present."

"Well, she is her own mistress, and I should not wish to alter her plans, but I shall be glad when I see her again. It is very lonely here without her company."

"I was afraid that you might find it so, and that was partly why I ran down. My young friend, Dr. Hamilton, is so much interested in the subject which you have made your own, that I thought you would not mind his accompanying me."

"I lead a retired life, Dr. Hamilton, and my aversion to strangers grows upon me," said our host. "I have sometimes thought that my nerves are not so good as they were. My travels in search of beetles in my younger days took me into many malarious and unhealthy places. But a brother coleopterist like yourself is always a welcome guest, and I shall be delighted if you will look over my collection, which I think that I may without exaggeration describe as the best in Europe."

And so no doubt it was. He had a huge, oaken cabinet arranged in shallow drawers, and here, neatly ticketed and classified, were beetles from every corner of the earth, black, brown, blue, green, and mottled. Every now and then as he swept his hand over the lines and lines of impaled insects he would catch up some rare specimen, and, handling it with as much delicacy and reverence as if it were a precious relic, he would hold forth upon its peculiarities and the circumstances under which it came into his possession. It was evidently an unusual thing for him to meet with a sympathetic listener, and he talked and talked until the spring evening had deepened into night, and the gong announced that it was time to dress for dinner. All the time Lord Linchmere said nothing, but he stood at his brother-in-law's elbow, and I caught him continually shooting curious little questioning glances into his face. And his own features expressed some strong emotion, apprehension, sympathy, expectation: I seemed to read them all. I was sure that Lord Linchmere was fearing something and awaiting something, but what that something might be I could not imagine.

The evening passed quietly but pleasantly, and I should have been entirely at my ease if it had not been for that continual sense of tension upon the part of Lord Linchmere. As to our host, I found that he improved upon acquaintance. He spoke constantly with affection of his absent wife, and also of his little son, who had recently been sent to school. The house, he said, was not the same without them. If it were not for his scientific studies, he did not know how he could get through the days. After dinner we smoked for some time in the billiard room, and finally went early to bed.

And then it was that, for the first time, the suspicion that Lord Linchmere was a lunatic crossed my mind. He followed me into my bedroom, when our host had retired.

"Doctor," said he, speaking in a low, hurried voice, "you must come with me. You must spend the night in my bedroom."

"What do you mean?"

"I prefer not to explain. But this is part of your duties. My room is close by, and you can return to your own before the servant calls you in the morning."

"But why?" I asked.

"Because I am nervous of being alone," said he. "That's the reason, since you must have a reason."

It seemed rank lunacy, but the argument of those 20 pounds would overcome many objections. I followed him to his room.

"Well," said I, "there's only room for one in that bed."

"Only one shall occupy it," said he.

"And the other?"

"Must remain on watch."

"Why?" said I. "One would think you expected to be attacked."

"Perhaps I do."

"In that case, why not lock your door?"

"Perhaps I want to be attacked."

It looked more and more like lunacy. However, there was nothing for it but to submit. I shrugged my shoulders and sat down in the armchair beside the empty fireplace.

"I am to remain on watch, then?" said I, ruefully.

"We will divide the night. If you will watch until two, I will watch the remainder."

"Very good."

"Call me at two o'clock, then."

"I will do so."

"Keep your ears open, and if you hear any sounds wake me instantly—instantly, you hear?"

"You can rely upon it." I tried to look as solemn as he did.

"And for God's sake don't go to sleep," said he, and so, taking off only his coat, he threw the coverlet over him and settled down for the night.

It was a melancholy vigil, and made more so by my own sense of its folly. Supposing that by any chance Lord Linchmere had cause to suspect that he was subject to danger in the house of Sir Thomas Rossiter, why on earth could he not lock his door and so protect himself? His own answer that he might wish to be attacked was absurd. Why should he possibly wish to be attacked? And who would wish to attack him? Clearly, Lord Linchmere was suffering from some singular delusion, and the result was that on an imbecile pretext I was to be deprived of my night's rest. Still, however absurd, I was determined to carry out his injunctions to the letter as long as I was in his employment. I sat, therefore, beside the empty fireplace, and listened to a sonorous chiming clock somewhere down the passage which gurgled and struck every quarter of an hour. It was an endless vigil. Save for that single clock, an absolute silence reigned throughout the great house. A small lamp stood on the table at my elbow, throwing a circle of light round my chair, but leaving the corners of the room draped in shadow. On the bed Lord Linchmere was breathing peacefully. I envied him his quiet sleep, and again and again my own eyelids drooped, but every time my sense of duty came to my help, and I sat up, rubbing my eyes and pinching myself with a determination to see my irrational watch to an end.

And I did so. From down the passage came the chimes of two o'clock, and I laid my hand upon the shoulder of the sleeper. Instantly he was sitting up, with an expression of the keenest interest upon his face.

"You have heard something?"

"No, sir. It is two o'clock."

"Very good. I will watch. You can go to sleep."

I lay down under the coverlet as he had done and was soon unconscious. My last recollection was of that circle of lamplight, and of the small, hunched-up figure and strained, anxious face of Lord Linchmere in the center of it.

How long I slept I do not know; but I was suddenly aroused by a sharp tug at my sleeve. The room was in darkness, but a hot smell of oil told me that the lamp had only that instant been extinguished.

"Quick! Quick!" said Lord Linchmere's voice in my ear.

I sprang out of bed, he still dragging at my arm.

"Over here!" he whispered, and pulled me into a corner of the room. "Hush! Listen!"

In the silence of the night I could distinctly hear that someone was coming down the corridor. It was a stealthy step, faint and intermittent, as of a man who paused cautiously after every stride. Sometimes for half a minute there was no sound, and then came the shuffle and creak which told of a fresh advance. My companion was trembling with excitement. His hand, which still held my sleeve, twitched like a branch in the wind.

"What is it?" I whispered.

"It's he!"

"Sir Thomas?"

"Yes."

"What does he want?"

"Hush! Do nothing until I tell you."

I was conscious now that someone was trying the door. There was the faintest little rattle from the handle, and then I dimly saw a thin slit of subdued light. There was a lamp burning somewhere far down the passage, and it just sufficed to make the outside visible from the darkness of our room. The grayish slit grew broader and broader, very gradually, very gently, and then outlined against it I saw the dark figure of a man. He was squat and crouching, with the silhouette of a bulky and misshapen dwarf. Slowly the door swung open with this ominous shape framed in the center of it. And then, in an instant, the crouching figure shot up, there was a tiger spring across the room and thud, thud, thud, came three tremendous blows from some heavy object upon the bed.

I was so paralyzed with amazement that I stood motionless and staring until I was aroused by a yell for help from my companion. The open door shed enough light for me to see the outline of things, and there was little Lord Linchmere with his arms round the neck of his brother-in-law, holding bravely onto him like a game bullterrier with its teeth into a gaunt deerhound. The tall, bony man dashed himself about, writhing round and round to get a grip upon his assailant; but the other, clutching on from behind, still kept his hold, though his shrill, frightened cries showed how unequal he felt the contest to be. I sprang to the rescue, and the two of us managed to throw Sir Thomas to the ground, though he made his teeth meet in my shoulder. With all my youth and weight and strength, it was a desperate struggle before we could master his frenzied struggles; but at last we secured his arms with the waist cord of the dressing gown which he was wearing. I was holding his legs while Lord Linchmere was endeavoring to relight the lamp, when there came the pattering of many feet in the passage, and the butler and two footmen, who had been alarmed by the cries, rushed into the room. With their aid we had no further difficulty in securing our prisoner, who lay foaming and glaring upon the ground. One glance at his face was enough to prove that he was a dangerous maniac, while the short, heavy hammer which lay beside the bed showed how murderous had been his intentions.

"Do not use any violence!" said Lord Linchmere, as we raised the struggling man to his feet. "He will have a period of stupor after this excitement. I believe that it is coming on already." As he spoke the convulsions became less violent, and the madman's head fell forward upon his breast, as if he were overcome by sleep. We led him down the passage and stretched him upon his own bed, where he lay unconscious, breathing heavily.

"Two of you will watch him," said Lord Linchmere. "And now, Dr. Hamilton, if you will return with me to my room, I will give you the explanation which my horror of scandal has perhaps caused me to delay too long. Come what may, you will never have cause to regret your share in this night's work.

"The case may be made clear in a very few words," he continued, when we were alone. "My poor brother-in-law is one of the best fellows upon earth, a loving husband and an estimable father, but he comes from a stock which is deeply tainted with insanity. He has more than once had homicidal outbreaks, which are the more painful because his inclination is always to attack the very person to whom he is most attached. His son was sent away to school to avoid this danger, and then came an attempt upon my sister, his wife, from which she escaped with injuries that you may have observed when you met her in London. You understand that he knows nothing of the matter when he is in his sound senses, and would ridicule the suggestion that he could under any circumstances injure those whom he loves so dearly. It is often, as you know, a characteristic of such maladies that it is absolutely impossible to convince the man who suffers from them of their existence.

"Our great object was, of course, to get him under restraint before he could stain his hands with blood, but the matter was full of difficulty. He is a recluse in his habits, and

74

would not see any medical man. Besides, it was necessary for our purpose that the medical man should convince himself of his insanity; and he is sane as you or I, save on these very rare occasions. But, fortunately, before he has these attacks he always shows certain premonitory symptoms, which are providential danger signals, warning us to be upon our guard. The chief of these is that nervous contortion of the forehead which you must have observed. This is a phenomenon which always appears from three to four days before his attacks of frenzy. The moment it showed itself his wife came into town on some pretext, and took refuge in my house in Brook Street.

"It remained for me to convince a medical man of Sir Thomas's insanity, without which it was impossible to put him where he could do no harm. The first problem was how to get a medical man into his house. I bethought me of his interest in beetles, and his love for anyone who shared his tastes. I advertised, therefore, and was fortunate enough to find in you the very man I wanted. A stout companion was necessary, for I knew that the lunacy could only be proved by a murderous assault, and I had every reason to believe that that assault would be made upon myself, since he had the warmest regard for me in his moments of sanity. I think your intelligence will supply all the rest. I did not know that the attack would come by night, but I thought it very probable, for the crises of such cases usually do occur in the early hours of the morning. I am a very nervous man myself, but I saw no other way in which I could remove this terrible danger from my sister's life. I need not ask you whether you are willing to sign the lunacy papers."

"Undoubtedly. But two signatures are necessary."

"You forget that I am myself a holder of a medical degree. I have the papers on a side table here, so if you will be good enough to sign them now, we can have the patient removed in the morning."

So that was my visit to Sir Thomas Rossiter, the famous beetle hunter, and that was also my first step upon the ladder of success, for Lady Rossiter and Lord Linchmere have proved to be staunch friends, and they have never forgotten my association with them in the time of their need. Sir Thomas is out and said to be cured, but I still think that if I spent another night at Delamere Court, I should be inclined to lock my door upon the inside.

THE BLACK NARCISSUS
Fred M. White
(1859-19??)

*Although it is easy to find biographical material about such authors
as Sir Arthur Conan Doyle and G. K. Chesterton, unearthing information about authors with shorter writing careers presents a challenge.
Hundreds of authors writing for the literary magazines of the day left
little to know about themselves save for their bylines. So it is with Fred
Merric White. We do know that White, an Englishman, was primarily
a writer of science fiction, although he wrote several fine detective stories
as well, including novels* Craven Fortune *(1908),* The Mystery of
the Ravenspurs *(1912), and the following tale.*

*What is so special about a black narcissus? Before the days
of modern plant breeding, black flowers were rare and much sought
after. Black is not a color nature chooses for flowers, since it doesn't
attract insects and other pollinators. The black flowers on the market
today have been created by plant breeders who begin with blue, red,
or purple flowers. If a flower such as the fictional black narcissus
truly existed, it might indeed inspire the kind of crime told in the
following tale!*

I

Twisting the card in his fingers, Lancaster Vane stood, impatient. He had all the novelist's scarring, lightning-flash passion for puerile interruption.

"Didn't I tell you?" he growled. Then he paused, with the surging sense of humor uppermost. The black-and-white starched parlor maid was wilting before his scathing indignation. "Don't you know that I once murdered a maid who disobeyed my orders like this? Show the man in."

The girl gurgled and vanished. Then followed a man with a gliding step and a moist gray eye, that took the whole room and the trim garden beyond and even the novelist in like the flash of a camera, and held the picture on the mental gelatin for all time.

"I am afraid I am intruding upon you, sir," the stranger suggested.

"Oh, you are," Vane said quietly. "Don't let that trouble you, though. I always work in the mornings, and I play golf all the afternoon. I make this arrangement so that if people waste my time in the mornings I can make up for it by sacrificing my pleasure after luncheon."

Inspector Darch, of Scotland Yard, ventured upon a smile.

"I come upon business of importance," he said.

"I guessed that from your card. Had you not been a policeman I should have declined to see you. In search of copy I have spent a deal of time in police and criminal courts, and I am bound to say I have a certain affection for the average constable. He has imagination—the way he generally gives his evidence shows that. He is a novelist in the nut."

Inspector Darch looked searchingly at the speaker. He was just a little disappointing. He was not tall and pale, with flashing eyes and long hair; on the contrary, his hair was that of the athlete, and he might have passed for a pugilist of the better class. The sensitive mouth and fine gray eyes saved the countenance from the commonplace. Thus it was that, after a second searching gaze, Darch seemed to see a face kaleidoscope from broad commonplace into the rugged suggestion of a young Gladstone. Here was no ordinary man. But then everybody who had studied Lancaster Vane's novels knew that.

"My complaint is, that we all lack imagination," the inspector said. "Of course, what you so playfully allude to is inventiveness. Young policemen always invent—they fancy that their first duty is to get a conviction. But they have no imagination. I've got a name and a good reputation, but no imagination."

"You have come to a deadlock in some case you have on hand?"

"That's it, sir. And I've made so bold as to come and ask for your assistance."

"Come out into the garden and smoke a cigar, then," Vane said suddenly.

Darch complied willingly. Vane's thatched cottage was on the river—a tiny place consisting of a large study, a smoking room, and a dining room, with quarters at the back for bachelor friends. Hither he had come earlier in the season than usual, with the intention of finishing a novel, before turning from "his beans and bacon," as he phrased it, to the butterfly delights of the London season. For Vane's books were satires for the most part, and he knew his world as well as any man living. Audacity and insight were the jewels in the wheel of his style. He had a marvelous faculty for seeing through a thing, a faculty that made him both respected and feared.

The garden was a riotous delight of daffodils and tulips, primulas and narcissus. There was no finer show of those pure spring flowers to be seen anywhere. Vane had a perfect passion for flowers, especially the spring varieties. He could name a bulb as a savant can locate the flint or the sandstone. With an eye for detail, Darch did not fail to notice that there were no less than 16 varieties of daffodils.

"Here I live for my work and my flowers," said Vane. "When down here, I smoke a pipe and live more or less on fish and bacon. When I am in town, I am nice over my wine and critical to rudeness over my friend's cigarettes. You are fond of flowers, Mr. Darch?"

"At present I am deeply interested in them," Darch replied.

"And thereby hangs a tale," said Vane. "Go on."

"There! I knew you were the man for me," Darch said admiringly.

Vane smiled; for even a novelist is only a man in disguise.

"Heavens! If I'd only got that insight of yours! It's a murder case, sir."

"You have a murder case on hand that utterly puzzles you?" Vane had dropped into a rustic garden seat, where he was thoughtfully pulling at his pipe. "And the matter is not remotely connected with flowers," he concluded.

"Got it again, sir!" the delighted Darch exclaimed. "You see, it's like this. I've read all your books—indeed, I have read most novels that make for the study of humanity, and I don't deny that I've learnt a lot that way."

"Have you, really?" Vane said quietly.

"I don't mind your little joke, sir. I've learnt that an innocent man can show exactly the same terror as the guilty caught red-handed; I've learnt—but no matter. And many a time it has struck me what a wonderful detective a first class novelist would make. I don't mean in little things, such as tracking criminals and the like—I mean in elucidating big problems. When we exhaust every avenue, his imagination would find a score of others, especially if he had a good psychological knowledge of his man. Now, I've got a case on hand that I believe you can solve for me, sir."

"Possibly," said Vane. "But where does my psychological knowledge come in? Seeing that there is no suspect, and that the victim is a stranger to me—"

"The victim is no stranger to you, Mr. Vane; I've found that out. And because you know him, and because of your novels, I am here today."

"This is getting interesting," Vane murmured. "The victim?"

"Ernst Van Noop. He was found dead in his cottage at Pinner last night, and there is not the slightest trace of the murderer. Van Noop lived in his house quite alone, and he seemed to have no hobby or occupation beyond his little garden and greenhouses."

"Except when he was spouting sedition in Hyde Park on Sundays," said Vane. "I'm sorry to hear about this. Really, Van Noop was a perfectly harmless creature, and at heart as gentle as a child. A little eccentric, but that was all."

Darch dissented mildly. He was bound to regard the doings of the dead Dutchman with an official eye. The man had been an anarchist of the worst type; his Sunday orations would never have been tolerated in any other country; his doctrines were, to say the least, inflammatory.

"You are quite wrong," said Vane. "Poor Van Noop would not have injured a fly. In his way the man was a genius, and genius must have an outlet, or it is apt to become chargeable upon the rates. Anarchy was Van Noop's safety valve. He and I came together over the common table of flowers—bulbs especially. He could have worked wonders in the way of hybrids and new varieties had he lived. Your dangerous character theory won't hold water. I defy you to prove to me that the poor old Dutchman consorted with notoriously dangerous characters."

"Then why did he ask for police protection?" Darch demanded. "What was he afraid of? He had no money or valuables, he never went near any of the Soho clubs; so far as we can tell, nobody suspicious ever went near him. Yet for the last few days that man has been frightened out of his life—afraid of being murdered, he said. At the same time he refused to give any account of the party or parties who held him in terror, and he point-blank declined to open his mouth as to the reason for any threats or danger."

"You fancy he was a Nihilist who had fallen under the ban of the order?"

"I feel practically certain of it, sir," Darch replied. "He has been murdered by those people, and they have left no trace behind. That is why I am here."

Vane smiled in a manner calculated to annoy anybody but a detective.

"I don't fancy you are far wrong to appeal to the imagination of a novelist," he said, "especially to a novelist who knows the victim. I don't know the murderer, any more than you do, but I'll prophesy for once. Within a week you shall have the assassin within your hands. Come, isn't that assertion enough even for a writer of fiction?"

"You can put your hand upon the Nihilist?" Darch cried. "You know him?"

"I don't know him, and he isn't a Nihilist," Vane replied. "I haven't the remotest idea who the murderer is, and yet I stick to my opinion. I am going entirely on a theory, which theory is built upon some knowledge of the dead man's past. You will, perhaps, be glad to hear that it is a theory that would only occur to a novelist; therefore you were perfectly right in the line of policy that brought you here. Now, perhaps you will be so good as to tell me all the details."

"The details are nil, practically," Darch replied. "The policeman on duty near Van Noop's cottage had certain special orders. He noticed that the door was not open late in the afternoon, and he could not make anybody hear. Then he burst open the door and found Van Noop lying dead in the kitchen with a wound in his side. There were no signs of violence; indeed, Van Noop must have been taken quite by surprise, for just under his heel, as if he had slipped upon it, was a small smashed onion."

"Onion!" Vane cried. "An onion! Great Scot!"

The mention of that homely yet pungent vegetable seemed to have the strangest effect upon the novelist. He glanced at Darch with mingled contempt and pity, a great agitation possessed him as he restlessly strode to and fro. Then he dropped into his seat again, and his shoulders shook in a fit of uncontrollable laughter.

"You will pardon me," he said, after a pause; "but your apparently commonplace words swept all the strings of emotion at once. And yet you say there is no clue. Now, could you have any clue stronger than an onion?"

"You are slightly too subtle for me, sir," Darch said, not without heat.

"I beg your pardon," Vane said contritely. "But I should very much like to see that onion."

Darch replied that the request might be complied with. He would have permitted himself the luxury of satire with any-body else but Vane over the matter. But then Vane had made him a cold, concrete promise that he should handle the quarry within seven days. From a novelist who had consistently refused to be interviewed, the promise carried weight.

"Was there anything else?" Vane asked.

"Nothing so prominent as the onion," Darch replied. "I, of course, made a close examination of the body, and in the right hand I found a flower. It looks to me like a periwinkle. Of course, it is much faded, and perhaps you may attach some importance to it. Being an ordinary man, it conveys nothing to me."

Vane's eyes were gleaming. The lines of his sensitive mouth twitched. If he was moved to laughter anymore, he laughed inside.

"I don't suppose it would," he said thoughtfully, "seeing that Van Noop was a lover of flowers. He might have been looking at the bloom at the moment when the fatal blow was struck. It would be quite natural for him to keep the flower in his grasp. You have it, of course?"

"Yes, sir," said Darch. "One never quite knows. Didn't some great man once say that there are no such things as small details?"

"Details are the cogwheels of great actions," Vane said sententiously. "Give me the flower."

Darch took the withered bloom from his pocketbook. It was wilted and lank, with a grass green stem and some dank velvet tassels hanging forlornly to the head. Had it been some precious treasure of the storied ages Vane could not have examined it more tenderly.

"What do you make of it?" Darch asked carelessly.

Vane shook his head. "The bloom is too far gone at present," he said. "It might be possible to revive it by plunging the whole into tepid water, with a little salt added." And yet, in spite of his assumed indifference, Vane's voice shook a little when he spoke.

"You had better leave this with me," he said. "In any case, it will be quite safe in my hands, and as the inquest on Van Noop's body is over, you will not need it for the present. At the same time, I am quite in earnest over my prophecy. If you will come here this day week at 6 P.M., I will go with you and assist you, if necessary, in arresting the murderer."

Darch departed, somewhat dazed at the result of his interview. But there was no smile on the face of the novelist, nothing but eager, palpitating curiosity, as he proceeded to plunge the wilted flower into water, to which a little salt was added.

"I'll go for a long pull on the river," he murmured. "I can't stay here by that thing. I should get an attack of nerves watching it expand. I wonder if it is possible that—"

He came back at length, two hours later, and proceeded to the study. Then he drew the flower from the water, and, behold! a glorious and pleasing transformation. The dead, crepe-like petals had filled out to a velvety, glossy softness, black as night and lustrous as ebony. There were five of these black petals, and in the center a calyx of deep purple with a heart of gold. Vane's hand shook as if with wine as he examined the perfect flowers, his eyes were glowing with admiration.

He flicked the water from it and dried it carefully. Then he held it where the sun might play upon the velvety luster and shine upon the perfect dead blackness. Vane's eyes were like those of a mother gazing at a child back from the gates of death.

"Now I know what Van Noop was hinting at," he said. "He said he had a fortune in his pocket, and he was right. And I am the only living man who has been as yet permitted to look upon a black narcissus."

II

It was characteristic of Lancaster Vane that he should throw himself heart and soul into his undertaking. It had occurred to him more than once that the typical detective officer was lacking in imagination, and crime in the abstract interested him, as it must interest all writers of fiction; and more than once he had found his theories of some great case not only at variance with the police, but absolutely right when they had been as absolutely wrong.

That marvelous audacity and insight had rarely failed Vane when dealing with living, breathing humanity. And he had no fear of failure here.

All the same, Inspector Darch began to grow uneasy when the sixth day came and nothing had transpired—at least, nothing of a tangible nature. He came down to the cottage late in the evening with a sufficiently flimsy excuse for seeing the man of letters.

Vane was seated in his study, reading by the light of a shaded lamp. The vivid bloodred line of the fringed silk was but one crimson spot in a dim, shimmering blackness. The novelist half sighed, and then smiled as he laid down his book.

"I had forgotten all about you, Darch," he said.

"You don't mean to say you have done nothing, sir?" the inspector cried.

"On the contrary, I have done a great deal, my friend," Vane replied. "I meant that I had forgotten you for a moment. I am reading a novel here which in my humble opinion is the best that Dumas ever wrote."

"*Monte Cristo?*" Darch murmured. "Hear, hear!"

"No, it is not *Monte Cristo,*" Vane replied. "I am alluding to *The Black Tulip.* Later on you will appreciate the value of the work. Imagination and education do a good deal for a man, but a judicious system of novel-reading does more. Some day our prophet shall arise and tell the world what an influence for good the best novels have wielded. Do you know the book?"

Darch admitted having skimmed it. He had found the characterization feeble—at least, from a detective's point of view. Vane smiled.

"I shall change your opinion presently," he said. "Have you discovered anything?"

"As to Van Noop, you mean? No, sir. Have you?"

"No," Vane replied. "I am still quite as much in the dark as yourself."

"But you promised me that within a week—"

"I would show you the man. Well, I am going to do so. I haven't the remotest idea who he is yet, but I am going to meet him tomorrow afternoon. When I have done so, I shall send you a telegram to Scotland Yard giving you the man's address and the hour you are to meet me there. Does that satisfy you?"

Darch expressed his thanks but feebly. All this was very irregular. Also, though it had an element of gasconade about it, it was impossible to look into Vane's strong, grave face and doubt that he believed every word that he uttered. If this were detective's work, why, then, it amounted to genius. And thus Darch departed, with a strong feeling of uncertainty.

It was a little after 12:00 the next day that Vane set out to walk from Pinner Station on the Metropolitan to the cottage recently inhabited by the unhappy Van Noop. Nearing his destination he felt in his pocketbook for certain news cuttings and a printed circular he had there. And this printed circular was to the effect that on this same date the whole of the garden produce, plants, flowers, bulbs, and apparatus generally belonging to the late Ernst Van Noop, were to be sold by auction, by order of the landlord, under a distress for rent. By the time Vane came to the cottage a free sprinkling of gardeners and florists had arrived, for, though the sale was a small one, Van Noop had been fairly well known amongst the brotherhood, and there was just the chance of picking up an odd parcel or so of hybrid bulbs which might become worth their weight in gold later on.

A lover of flowers and a man keen on anything new in that direction, Vane was respectfully recognized. Most of the dealers present were gathered in the kitchen of the cottage where the bulbs were set out in little coarse blue paper bags. Most of them were properly labeled and cataloged, but there were three packets, of four bulbs each, to which the most trained florist present would have found it hard to give a name.

Vane pushed his way through a little knot of dealers. One of them touched his hat.

"Anything new here, Harris?" he asked.

"Well, sir," was the reply. "Van Noop was a close sort of party. I did hear something—in fact, I read it in the *Garden Herald* today—as Van Noop had some wonderful black bulbs here, but maybe it's all nonsense. I can't make head or tail of those little packets yonder, and I should be sorry to risk a sovereign on the chance of them turning out anything beyond the common. The other bulbs look good, but we could all show as fine a variety."

"I'll speculate," said Vane. "There's a commission for you, Harris. You can go up to five pounds each for those particular packets, but not a penny beyond. Of course, it will be throwing money away; but nothing venture, nothing win. And it may be possible that the *Garden Herald* was right, and Van Noop had invented the black tulip, after all."

Vane had spoken loud enough for everybody to hear. Then he left the cottage and strode down with the air of a man who has important business before him. He came back later and lounged into the cottage unconcernedly with a pipe in his mouth. The small knot of buyers were still lingering there. Vane came up to Harris languidly.

"Well," he asked. "Do you want my check for those mysterious bulbs?"

"No, sir," Harris replied, "and in my opinion you're quite well out of it. I bid up to five pounds, and then a stranger raised me a sovereign a bag, and I dropped it, of course. There he is, sir. You don't often get a chance to see the amateur enthusiast at his best; but he's only a foreigner."

This with the finest insular contempt. Vane glanced carelessly at the slight, stooping figure and thin, pinched features of the man who had incurred the florist's displeasure. The eyes he could not see, for they were behind glasses.

"Evidently an enthusiast, like myself," Vane said. "We all have our philosopher's stone, Harris."

"I dare say we do," Harris replied sententiously.

Vane smiled again. He passed over to the auctioneer and, after a few minutes with that worthy, scribbled out a telegram in pencil. When he looked round again, the foreign connoisseur had disappeared. Harris was busily engaged in directing the package of his own small purchase.

"I am coming over tomorrow to see that salmon auricula of yours," said Vane. "I am sorry to say that mine are doing indifferently. Not enough shade, perhaps."

"That's it, sir," Harris responded. "Aristocratic flower, naturally, is the auricula. Put 'em in an old garden along the borders under apple trees, and you can grow 'em like peonies. It's only county people who can grow auriculas."

"I'll put a coat-of-arms over mine," Vane laughed. "By the way, as you are passing a station, will you be good enough to send this telegram for me?"

The telegram merely contained an address, followed by a single figure, and was directed to Darch's registered address at Scotland Yard. To the casual reader it conveyed nothing. Then Vane made his way into the road.

He walked on for a mile or more until he came, at length, to a pretty little cottage, a double-fronted one-story affair, covered with creepers. There was a long garden in front, a garden deep sunken between trim, thick hedges, the black soil of which was studded with thousands of flowers—hyacinths, tulips, narcissus, nothing was wanting.

Vane's artistic eye reveled in the lovely sight.

He stood thus feasting his soul on the mass of beautiful colors before him. The more important mission was forgotten for the moment. There was something of envy in Vane's glance, too, for with all his lavish outlay he could not produce blooms like these. And the owner of the place was obviously a poor man.

"A better soil, perhaps," Vane muttered, "or perhaps it's because these beauties get the whole attention of the grower. Flowers want more attention than most women. When those gladiolus come into bloom—"

Vane paused in his ruminations as the owner of the cottage came out. He had a black velvet skullcap on the back of his head, around which gray hairs straggled like a thatch. As he stood in the path of the setting sun Vane noticed the long, slender hands and a heavy signet ring on the right little finger. They were not the hands of the toiler or workman, and yet to Vane they indicated both strength and resolution.

"I am admiring your flowers," he said. "They are absolutely perfect. I am an enthusiast myself, but I have nothing like this."

"Nothing so perfect?" the old man said. "Won't you come in, sir?"

The question was asked with a certain mixture of humility and high courtesy that seemed to take Vane back over the bridge of the centuries. The man before him was bent and shaken by the palsy of old age, and yet his eyes were full of fire and determination. His English was thin and foreign, yet he spoke with the easy fluency of the scholar. Again Vane forgot his mission. An hour or more passed, the sun had flamed down behind the fragrant hawthorn, and Vane was still listening.

He had met a man with an enthusiasm greater than his own. Vane was standing in the presence of a master, and he knew it. The man was talking excitedly.

"I was a rich man once," he said. "The Van Eykes were a power in Holland at one time. And I have ruined myself over flowers as Orientals ruin themselves over their harems, and as the visionary in seeking for the elixir of life. Flowers have ever been my mistress—I have given my all for them, my life to the study of the secrets of nature. If I could only go down to posterity as the inventor of something new—"

"A black tulip, for instance," Vane suggested.

The dark eyes behind the glasses flashed. Vane looked at his watch.

"Oh, yes!" Van Eyke cried. "It was that fascinating romance that first set me thinking. Perhaps you, too, have had your dreams, sir?"

"I confess it," Vane smiled. "You see, I am a novelist as well as a florist. I am still sanguine of seeing a black, a velvety black, flower. It will be soft-stemmed when it comes, and, as you know, it will be a bulbous plant."

"Perhaps I shall be able to show it to you."

Van Eyke spoke quietly, yet with a thrill in his voice. His hand trembled with something more than the weight of years. His glance wandered toward the house.

"I had it almost within my grasp five years ago," he said. "I was living near Amsterdam then. You should have seen my hybrids—black, and white, and patches, and the black predominating. Heavens! how I longed and waited for the next springtime!"

"You are speaking of tulips, of course?" Vane asked carelessly.

"Oh, no," said Van Eyke. He paused in confusion, the red thread of his lips paled. "Yes, yes, of course I meant tulips. The black tulip. Ah, ah!"

His gaiety was not a pleasant thing. It was too suggestive of the butterfly on the skeleton.

"Oh! I waited for the springtime," he went on. "Aye, I waited as a prisoner for freedom. And they all came pink! My children had been stolen! Sir, you are a novelist. You can understand the frame of mind in which one commits murder."

"Did you track the man who had robbed you?" Vane asked.

"After a time I did; but it was years. Sir, I am talking nonsense."

"You may have said too much in the excitement of the moment," Vane said coolly, "but certainly you are not talking nonsense. You tracked your man, and you killed him. Why?"

Van Eyke's hands went up with an almost mechanical gesture. At the same moment a step was heard, crunching the gravel outside, and Darch appeared. Vane made a motion with his hand in the direction of Van Eyke's bent, quivering figure.

"You have come in time," he said. "This is Mr. Darch, of Scotland Yard. And this is Mr. Van Eyke, the man who killed Van Noop a few days ago."

Darch was too astonished to speak for a moment. The dramatic force of the situation had almost overpowered him. For crime as a rule is sordid enough, and the heroic in the life of a detective is only for the pages of fiction.

"This is a poor return for all my courtesy," Van Eyke said, not without dignity. "I have never even heard of the gentleman you mention."

Darch looked helplessly at Vane. The suggestion that he was about to be fooled was painful. Never had the mantle of the majesty of the law lain more awkwardly on his shoulders.

"It is quite possible," Vane said, "that you never heard of Van Noop by that name. But assuredly you knew all about the man at Pinner, the man who was murdered, and some of whose bulbs today fetched over five pounds a packet, or nearly two pounds per bulb."

"I have not heard of that," said Van Eyke.

"Strange, seeing that you purchased them," Vane went on. "This is nonsense, Mr. Van Eyke. I saw you at the sale, and I am surprised that you did not see me. However, all this is beside the point. You bought those bulbs at an extravagant price because you believed that they were the bulbs of the black—"

"There is not a black—a black tulip in the world."

"Who said anything about a black tulip?" Vane retorted. "What you were after was a black narcissus. Perhaps you will deny the existence of that?"

"I should like to see it, above all things."

The sneer passed over Vane's head. He stepped close to Van Eyke and opened his overcoat. In the lapel of his coat, the stem carefully preserved in water, he wore Van Noop's black narcissus. The flower was slightly ragged at the edges, but it was all there, like a lovely woman past her prime.

The effect was staggering. Van Eyke fell, as if some unseen power had beaten him to his knees.

"Where did you get it?" he asked hoarsely. "Where did you get it?"

"Surely you need not ask the question," said Vane. "It was the one Van Noop was holding in his hand at the time you murdered him."

Van Eyke rose slowly to his feet. He made no further denial of the grave charge, he seemed to be absolutely unconscious of the danger hanging over his head. He had only eyes for the flower in Vane's coat. Darch watched the scene with lively admiration.

"Let me see it, let me hold it," said Van Eyke. He spoke like a man in a dream. "I don't care what you do, I don't care what happens to me, so long as I can hold that flower in my hand. You need not be afraid. I will not injure it. Injure it? Bah! Would a mother injure her firstborn? I have sold my soul for it, as Faust sold his for Marguerite."

His eyes had grown soft and pleading. It seemed impossible to believe that the gentle, quivering creature could have the blood of a fellow creature on his hands. Vane passed the flower over, in spite of a glance of disapproval from Darch. It seemed like madness to hand over to the prisoner's custody the strongest link of evidence against him and how frail that link was!

Van Eyke bent over the flower and pressed it to his lips.

"This is mine," he said, "mine! For 20 years I have labored to attain this result. Another hand grew it, another hand feuded it and fostered it, but the child is mine. Van Noop stole my black and white hybrids two years ago, and from them he has developed this. He has been no more than the clod who has made the frame and varnished the canvas, for the picture is mine. And I killed him."

The confession was out at last. Darch stepped forward. The man was merged in the official. For the moment he forgot to admire Vane and the wonderful way in which he had elucidated the mystery. He became a mere detective again.

"I must warn you," he said, "that all you say will be taken in evidence against you."

Van Eyke smiled. Then he handed the black narcissus back to Vane. "What does it matter?" he said. "What does anything matter? I have seen all the fond hopes of years grati-fied, and I can die happy. I care nothing whatever whether Van Noop or myself gets the credit for the black narcissus, so long as it is there. He robbed me—I found him—and I killed him—killed him with the very thing I coveted in his hand. He died with it in his hand, and I never knew it.

"It is two years since I tracked Van Noop to England, after he robbed me. Then I settled down in this cottage, waiting my time, and for two years he lived within a mile of me, and I never knew it—never found it out. A month last Sunday I was in London. I was passing through Hyde Park when I heard an anarchist addressing a mob. Something in his voice impelled me to draw near. It was my man, the man who had robbed me of the best part of my life.

"I followed him home. I found where he lived, and I waited my opportunity. It came. I slipped into the cottage when the door was open, and there he was, bending over a pot with a flower growing in it. I made a noise, and he turned and saw me. I fancied that it was his fear that caused him to break off the flower in the pot, but I had only eyes for my foe. Then with a knife I struck him to the heart, and he died without a murmur. For an hour I remained there, searching the house, but I could not find what I was search-ing for. I was looking for the black narcissus. Gentlemen, that is all."

"One question," said Vane. "Had you been hanging about Van Noop's cottage?"

"For three or four weeks, yes," Van Eyke replied. "I was seeking for my opportunity."

"Is it possible that he might have discovered this?"

"Oh, it is possible, all these things are possible. Why?"

"I was merely asking for my own information," said Vane. "There was a point to be cleared up, and you have done it for us. I am sorry for this, very sorry. It seems a pity that so fine and innocent and beautiful a place should be mixed up in a sordid crime like this."

Van Eyke shrugged his shoulders. There was no trace of fear in his eyes now; indeed, it seemed to Vane that those eyes were blazing with a fire beyond the bright glow of reason.

"Most of the brightest jewels in the world are stained with blood," Van Eyke said, "and if the orchids in your millionaires' houses could speak, what tragedies they might tell! Sir, I am in your hands. Sir, I wish you good night."

The Dutchman turned from Darch to Vane with a stately courtesy. He might have been a lordly host bowing out two objectionable visitors. A little later, and the prisoner found himself with a stolid policeman in the back of a dog cart. Darch lingered a moment before he took his seat.

"Mr. Vane," he said, "this is really wonderful."

"It is exceedingly painful and squalid to me," Vane replied. "But I see you are puzzled. You have seen the problem finished, and naturally you are anxious to have the moves all explained. If you will come to the Lotus Club after dinner tomorrow night, I will make everything clear. Say nine o'clock."

"Mr. Vane," Darch said emphatically, "I will be there."

III

"And now, Darch," said Vane, as he finished his coffee daintily, "I am going to be egotistical. I am going to talk about myself to the extent of some one thousand words As a rule, I get some 20 guineas per thousand for my words—but that is another story.

"The other night you came to me with a story of an anarchist who asked for police protection, because—so you imagined—he had done something wrong in the eyes of other Nihilists, and feared for his life. You came to me, in the first place, to obtain inspiration from a novelist, and, secondly, because the victim was, like myself, an ardent lover of flowers.

"Now, in the first place, permit me to correct a wrong impression of yours. From your point of view I should never make a good detective. I decline to believe in the theory of obvious deduction. Dupin and Sherlock Holmes were steeped to the lips in it. My word! What blunders they would have made had they reduced those theories to practice! Holmes takes a watch, and from a keyhole, by the scratches, deduces that the owner is a man of dissipated habits. But suppose he had been partially blind or suffering, from paralysis, eh? No, that's no good save in fiction.

"Now, I knew Van Noop. I knew him to be incapable of injuring a fly. His socialism was merely a safety valve. The man might have been a visionary, but what he didn't know about flowers wasn't worth knowing. And more than once he had hinted to me that he was on the verge of a great discovery. As bulbs were his hobby, and as he was a Dutchman, also, as he was a great admirer of Dumas, I guessed he was after a black flower. They are all after it. And it was not to be a tulip, because Van Noop didn't care much for tulips.

"Then you came to me and told me he had been murdered. You told me about the mysterious way in which he had asked for police protection, and instantly it flashed across my mind that somebody had discovered his secret and was trying to get it from him. When you brought me that withered flower, I was sure of my argument; and when you spoke of that smashed onion, I was positive. You made me laugh over that onion, you remember. That probably was a bulb of the black narcissus, though as a layman you were quite justified in taking it for that succulent vegetable.

"After you were gone I developed the black narcissus. There before me was a motive for the murder. It seemed to me that there had been a struggle for it, and that Van Noop had destroyed the flower and crushed the bulb just before he was killed. Then, as a natural sequence to this important discovery, the story of *The Black Tulip* came into my mind. I had to find the man who committed the crime for the sake of the narcissus. And this is where the novelist comes in. It was not a case for obvious deduction, it was a case of introspection. You would have gone on blundering your head against Nihilist revenge and the like. I simply had to weave a romance round that flower, a romance with blood in it. And gradually my art and my imagination led me to the true and only possible solution of the mystery. Van Noop had been murdered for the sake of the black narcissus beyond question, and the assassin must be an enthusiast and a madman, like himself. You will call all this intuition.

"Then I had to draw my man. I found out when the sale was coming off, and a man who knows the address of every amateur gardener in London posted a special circular I had printed hinting that Van Noop's collection held rare things to buyers. When I reached Van Noop's cottage on the day of the sale I had no idea who the murderer was, but I felt absolutely certain that he would be present, whether he had my circular or not. Then, in a stage whisper, I asked a florist to purchase a parcel or two of bulbs for me at a fancy price. As I expected, on my return I found they had been bought over my head by somebody else. And then, my dear Darch, I knew the man who had murdered Van Noop. I had only to go over to the auctioneer and obtain the address of the man who had given a large sum for a parcel of bulbs which he fondly hoped contained the black narcissus. I obtained that address and followed Van Eyke to his cottage."

"Wonderful!" Darch cried. "I should never have thought of it."

"Of course you wouldn't," Vane replied. "Crime for crime's sake would be the only motive that appealed to you. And why? Because it is impossible for the detective trained in the ordinary way to appreciate or understand the poetic side of crime. And yet I defy you to find anything sordid in the case. The whole thing is absolutely medieval. In this prosaic age it seems extraordinary that a man should commit murder for the sake of a flower. And yet in Van Eyke you have a man who would not have shed a drop of blood for all the mines of Golconda."

"You are right, sir," said Darch thoughtfully; "and I was right also. I knew that a man of imagination would be required here, and I found him. And I don't mind confessing that I should never have dreamt of connecting that crime with a simple flower."

"You might," Vane replied. "When everything else failed, you would probably have started to look out for the owner of the flower, going on the theory that the dead man had snatched it from the coat of the murderer. Another time, perhaps, I may show you how my detective theory can be worked out in another fashion. And the next time you find an onion, be quite sure it is an onion, and not a priceless bulb worth a king's ransom."

The Arrest of Arsène Lupin
from *Arsène Lupin—Gentleman Burglar*
Maurice Leblanc

Maurice Leblanc, son of the wealthy owner of a shipping firm, was born in Rouen, France. He was educated in France, Germany, and Italy. He went to work for the family firm but soon grew bored of the shipping business. Writing was his greater interest. He abandoned the family business to become a journalist and a writer of pulp crime fiction. Leblanc's first works appeared in such Paris newspapers as Echo de Paris. *His first novel,* Une Femme (A Woman), *was published in 1887. It was a psychological piece that achieved only modest success.*

Leblanc continued writing articles and stories for the newspapers and periodicals of Paris for many years. Fame came quite by accident when a casual assignment from the journal, Je Sais Tout *(literally: "I Know All"), lead to Leblanc's creation of a fictional gentleman burglar, Arsène Lupin (pronounced Lu-pahn). The character was an immediate hit. For the next 25 years, Leblanc continued writing Lupin stories, which became nearly as popular as the Sherlock Holmes adventures.*

The first Lupin novel, Arsène Lupin, Gentleman Cambrioleur, *was published in 1907. The tale below is Leblanc's first short story featuring Arsène Lupin. Note Lupin's inimitable character even in this first tale, how he attempted to burgle a rich man's house, but in the end, took nothing and left a note saying he would return "when the furniture is genuine."*

It was a strange ending to a voyage that had commenced in a most auspicious manner. The transatlantic steamship *La Provence* was a swift and comfortable vessel, under the command of a most affable man. The passengers constituted a select and delightful society. The charm of new acquaintances and improvised amusements served to make the time pass agreeably. We enjoyed the pleasant sensation of being separated from the world, living, as it were, upon an unknown island, and consequently obliged to be sociable with each other.

Have you ever stopped to consider how much originality and spontaneity emanate from these various individuals who, on the preceding evening, did not even know each other, and who are now, for several days, condemned to lead a life of extreme intimacy, jointly defying the anger of the ocean, the terrible onslaught of the waves, the violence of the tempest and the agonizing monotony of the calm and sleepy water? Such a life becomes a sort of tragic existence, with its storms and its grandeurs, its monotony and its diversity; and that is why, perhaps, we embark upon that short voyage with mingled feelings of pleasure and fear.

But, during the past few years, a new sensation has been added to the life of the transatlantic traveler. The little floating island is now attached to the world from which it was once quite free. A bond unites them, even in the very heart of the watery wastes of the Atlantic. That bond is the wireless telegraph, by means of which we receive news in the most mysterious manner. We know full well that the message is not transported by the medium of a hollow wire. No, the mystery is even more inexplicable, more romantic, and we must have recourse to the wings of the air in order to explain this new miracle. During the first day of the voyage, we felt that we were followed, escorted, preceded even, by that distant voice, which, from time to time, whispered to one of us a few words from the receding world. Two friends spoke to me. Ten, twenty others sent merry or somber words of parting to other passengers.

On the second day, at a distance of five hundred miles from the French coast, in the midst of a violent storm, we received the following message by means of the wireless telegraph:

> Arséne Lupin is on your vessel, first cabin, blond hair, wound right forearm, traveling alone under name of R.

At that moment, a terrible flash of lightning rent the stormy skies. The electric waves were interrupted. The remainder of the dispatch never reached us. Of the name under which Arséne Lupin was concealing himself, we knew only the initial.

If the news had been of some other character, I would have no doubt that the secret would have been carefully guarded by the telegraphic operator as well as by the officers of the vessel. But it was one of those events calculated to escape from the most rigorous discretion. The same day, no one knew how, the incident became a matter of current gossip and every passenger was aware that the famous Arséne Lupin was hiding in our midst.

Arséne Lupin in our midst! The irrepressible burglar whose exploits had been narrated in all the newspapers during the past few months! The mysterious individual with whom Ganimard, our shrewdest detective, had been engaged in an implacable conflict amidst interesting and picturesque surroundings. Arséne Lupin, the eccentric gentleman who operates only in the chateaux and salons, and who, one night, entered the residence of Baron Schormann, but emerged empty-handed, leaving, however, his card on which he had scribbled these words: "Arséne Lupin, gentleman-burglar, will return when the furniture is genuine." Arséne Lupin, the man of a thousand disguises: in turn a chauffeur, detective, bookmaker, Russian physician, Spanish bull-fighter, commercial traveler, robust youth, or decrepit old man.

Then consider this startling situation: Arséne Lupin was wandering about within the limited bounds of a transatlantic steamer; in that very small corner of the world, in that dining saloon, in that smoking room, in that music room! Arséne Lupin was, perhaps, this gentleman . . . or that one . . . my neighbor at the table . . . the sharer of my stateroom.

"And this condition of affairs will last for five days!" exclaimed Miss Nelly Underdown, next morning. "It is unbearable! I hope he will be arrested."

Then, addressing me, she added: "And you, Monsieur d'Andrezy, you are on intimate terms with the captain; surely you know something?"

I should have been delighted had I possessed any information that would interest Miss Nelly. She was one of those magnificent creatures who inevitably attract attention in every assembly. Wealth and beauty form an irresistible combination, and Nelly possessed both.

Educated in Paris under the care of a French mother, she was now going to visit her father, the millionaire Underdown of Chicago. She was accompanied by one of her friends, Lady Jerland.

At first, I had decided to open a flirtation with her; but, in the rapidly growing intimacy of the voyage, I was soon impressed by her charming manner and my feelings became too deep and reverential for a mere flirtation. Moreover, she accepted my attentions with a certain degree of favor. She condescended to laugh at my witticisms and display an interest in my stories. Yet I felt that I had a rival in the person of a young man with quiet and refined tastes; and it struck me, at times, that she preferred his taciturn humor to my Parisian frivolity. He formed one in the circle of admirers that surrounded Miss Nelly at the time she addressed to me the foregoing question. We were all comfortably seated in our deck chairs. The storm of the preceding evening had cleared the sky. The weather was now delightful.

"I have no definite knowledge, mademoiselle," I replied, "but cannot we, ourselves, investigate the mystery quite as well as the detective Ganimard, the personal enemy of Arséne Lupin?"

"Oh! Oh! You are progressing very fast, monsieur."

"Not at all, mademoiselle. In the first place, let me ask, do you find the problem a complicated one?"

"Very complicated."

"Have you forgotten the key we hold for the solution of the problem? "

"What key?"

"In the first place, Lupin calls himself Monsieur R."

"Rather vague information," she replied.

"Secondly, he is traveling alone."

"Does that help you?" she asked.

"Thirdly, he is blond."

"Well? "

"Then we have only to peruse the passenger list, and proceed by the process of elimination."

I had that list in my pocket. I took it out and glanced through it. Then I remarked: "I find that there are only thirteen men on the passenger list whose names begin with the letter R."

"Only thirteen?"

"Yes, in the first cabin. And of those thirteen, I find that nine of them are accompanied by women, children or servants. That leaves only four who are traveling alone. First, the Marquis de Raverdan—"

"Secretary to the American ambassador," interrupted Miss Nelly. "I know him."

"Major Rawson," I continued.

"He is my uncle," someone said.

"Monsieur Rivolta."

"Here!" exclaimed an Italian, whose face was concealed beneath a heavy black beard.

Miss Nelly burst into laughter, and exclaimed: "That gentleman can scarcely be called a blond."

"Very well, then," I said, "we are forced to the conclusion that the guilty party is the last one on the list."

"What is his name?"

"Monsieur Rozaine. Does anyone know him?"

No one answered. But Miss Nelly turned to the taciturn young man, whose attentions to her had annoyed me, and said: "Well, Monsieur Rozaine, why do you not answer?"

All eyes were now turned upon him. He was a blond. I must confess that I myself felt a shock of surprise, and the profound silence that followed her question indicated that the others present also viewed the situation with a feeling of sudden alarm. However, the idea was an absurd one, because the gentleman in question presented an air of the most perfect innocence.

"Why do I not answer?" he said. "Because, considering my name, my position as a solitary traveler and the color of my hair, I have already reached the same conclusion, and now think that I should be arrested."

He presented a strange appearance as he uttered these words. His thin lips were drawn closer than usual and his face was ghastly pale, whilst his eyes were streaked with blood. Of course, he was joking, yet his appearance and attitude impressed us strangely.

"But you have not the wound?" said Miss Nelly, naively.

"That is true," he replied, "I lack the wound."

Then he pulled up his sleeve, removing his cuff, and showed us his arm. But that action did not deceive me. He had shown us his left arm, and I was on the point of calling his attention to the fact, when another incident diverted our attention. Lady Jerland, Miss Nelly's friend, came running toward us in a state of great excitement, exclaiming: "My jewels, my pearls! Someone has stolen them all!"

No, they were not all gone, as we soon found out. The thief had taken only part of them; a very curious thing. Of the diamond sunbursts, jeweled pendants, bracelets and necklaces, the thief had taken, not the largest but the finest and most valuable stones. The mountings were lying upon the table. I saw them there, despoiled of their jewels, like flowers from which the beautiful colored petals had been ruthlessly plucked. And this theft must have been committed at the time Lady Jerland was taking her tea; in broad daylight, in a stateroom opening on a much-frequented corridor; moreover, the thief had been obliged to force open the door of the stateroom, search for the jewel case, which was hidden at the bottom of a hatbox, open it, select his booty and remove it from the mountings.

Of course, all the passengers instantly reached the same conclusion; it was the work of Arséne Lupin.

That day, at the dinner table, the seats to the right and left of Rozaine remained vacant; and, during the evening, it was rumored that the captain had placed him under arrest, which information produced a feeling of safety and relief. We breathed once more. That evening, we resumed our games and dances. Miss Nelly, especially, displayed a spirit of thoughtless gaiety which convinced me that if Rozaine's attentions had been agreeable to her in the beginning, she had already forgotten them. Her charm and good humor completed my conquest. At midnight, under a bright moon, I declared my devotion with an ardor that did not seem to displease her.

But next day, to our general amazement, Rozaine was at liberty. We learned that the evidence against him was not sufficient. He had produced documents that were perfectly regular, which showed that he was the son of a wealthy merchant of Bordeaux. Besides, his arms did not bear the slightest trace of a wound.

"Documents! Certificates of birth!" exclaimed the enemies of Rozaine. "Of course, Arséne Lupin will furnish you as many as you desire. And as to the wound, he never had it, or he has removed it."

Then it was proven that, at the time of the theft, Rozaine was promenading on the deck. To which fact his enemies replied that a man like Arséne Lupin could commit a crime without being actually present. And then, apart from all other circumstances, there remained one point which even the most skeptical could not answer: Who except Rozaine was traveling alone, was a blond, and bore a name beginning with R? To whom did the telegram point, if it were not Rozaine?

And when Rozaine, a few minutes before breakfast, came boldly toward our group, Miss Nelly and Lady Jerland arose and walked away.

An hour later a manuscript circular was passed from hand to hand amongst the sailors, the stewards, and the passengers of all classes. It announced that Monsieur Louis Rozaine offered a reward of 10,000 francs for the discovery of Arséne Lupin or other person in possession of the stolen jewels.

"And if no one assists me, I will unmask the scoundrel myself," declared Rozaine.

Rozaine against Arséne Lupin, or, rather, according to current opinion, Arséne Lupin himself against Arséne Lupin; the contest promised to be interesting.

Nothing developed during the next two days. We saw Rozaine wandering about, day and night, searching, questioning, investigating. The captain also displayed commendable activity. He caused the vessel to be searched from stem to stern, ransacked every stateroom under the plausible theory that the jewels might be concealed anywhere, except in the thief's own room.

"I suppose they will find out something soon," remarked Miss Nelly to me. "He may be a wizard, but he cannot make the diamonds and pearls become invisible."

"Certainly not," I replied, "but he should examine the lining of our hats and vests and everything we carry with us."

Then, exhibiting my Kodak, a 9 x 12 with which I had been photographing her in various poses, I added: "In an apparatus no larger than that a person could hide all of Lady Jerland's jewels. He could pretend to take pictures and no one would suspect the game."

"But I have heard it said that every thief leaves some clue behind him."

"That may be generally true," I replied, "but there is one exception: Arséne Lupin."

"Why?"

"Because he concentrates his thoughts not only on the theft, but on all the circumstances connected with it that could serve as a clue to his identity."

"A few days ago, you were more confident."

"Yes, but since then I have seen him at work."

"And what do you think about it now?" she asked.

"Well, in my opinion, we are wasting our time."

And, as a matter-of-fact, the investigation had produced no result. But in the meantime the captain's watch had been stolen. He was furious. He quickened his efforts and watched Rozaine more closely than before. But, on the following day, the watch was found in the second officer's collar box.

This incident caused considerable astonishment, and displayed the humorous side of Arséne Lupin, burglar though he was, but dilettante as well. He combined business with pleasure. He reminded us of the author who almost died in a fit of laughter provoked by his own play. Certainly, he was an artist in his peculiar line of work, and whenever I saw Rozaine, gloomy and reserved, and thought of the double role that he was playing, I accorded him a certain measure of admiration.

On the following evening, the officer on deck duty heard groans emanating from the darkest corner of the ship. He approached and found a man lying there, his head enveloped in a thick gray scarf and his hands tied together with a heavy cord. It was Rozaine. He had been assaulted, thrown down and robbed. A card, pinned to his coat, bore these words: "Arséne Lupin accepts with pleasure the 10,000 francs offered by Monsieur Rozaine." As a matter of fact, the stolen pocket-book contained 20,000 francs.

Of course, some accused the unfortunate man of having simulated this attack on himself. But, apart from the fact that he could not have bound himself in that manner, it was established that the writing on the card was entirely different from that of Rozaine, but, on the contrary, resembled the handwriting of Arséne Lupin as it was reproduced in an old newspaper found on board.

Thus it appeared that Rozaine was not Arséne Lupin but was Rozaine, the son of a Bordeaux merchant. And the presence of Arséne Lupin was once more affirmed, and that in a most alarming manner.

Such was the state of terror amongst the passengers that none would remain alone in a stateroom or wander singly in unfrequented parts of the vessel. We clung together as a matter of safety. And yet the most intimate acquaintances were estranged by a mutual feeling of distrust. Arséne Lupin was, now, anybody and everybody. Our excited imaginations attributed to him miraculous and unlimited power. We supposed him capable of assuming the most unexpected disguises; of being, by turns, the highly respectable Major Rawson or the noble Marquis de Raverdan, or even—for we no longer stopped with the accusing letter R—or even such or such a person well known to all of us, and having wife, children and servants.

The first wireless dispatches from America brought no news; at least, the captain did not communicate any to us. The silence was not reassuring.

Our last day on the steamer seemed interminable. We lived in constant fear of some disaster. This time, it would not be a simple theft or a comparatively harmless assault; it would be a violent crime, a murder. No one imagined that Arséne Lupin would confine himself to those two trifling offenses. Absolute master of the ship, the authorities powerless, he could do whatever he pleased; our property and lives were at his mercy.

Yet those were delightful hours for me, since they secured to me the confidence of Miss Nelly. Deeply moved by those startling events and being of a highly nervous nature, she spontaneously sought at my side a protection and security that I was pleased to give her. Inwardly, I blessed Arséne Lupin. Had he not been the means of bringing me and Miss Nelly closer to each other? Thanks to him, I could now indulge in delicious dreams of love and happiness—dreams that, I felt, were not unwelcome to Miss Nelly. Her smiling eyes authorized me to make them; the softness of her voice bade me hope.

As we approached the American shore, the active search for the thief was apparently abandoned, and we were anxiously awaiting the supreme moment in which the mysterious enigma would be explained. Who was Arséne Lupin? Under what name, under what disguise was the famous Arséne Lupin concealing himself? And, at last, that supreme moment arrived. If I live 100 years, I shall not forget the slightest detail of it.

"How pale you are, Miss Nelly," I said to my companion, as she leaned upon my arm, almost fainting.

"And you!" she replied. "Ah, you are so changed."

"Just think! This is a most exciting moment, and I am delighted to spend it with you, Miss Nelly. I hope that your memory will sometimes revert—"

But she was not listening. She was nervous and excited. The gangway was placed in position, but, before we could use it, the uniformed customs officers came on board. Miss Nelly murmured: "I shouldn't be surprised to hear that Arséne Lupin escaped from the vessel during the voyage."

"Perhaps he preferred death to dishonor, and plunged into the Atlantic rather than be arrested."

"Oh, do not laugh," she said.

Suddenly I started, and, in answer to her question, I said: "Do you see that little old man standing at the bottom of the gangway?"

"With an umbrella and an olive-green coat?"

"It is Ganimard."

"Ganimard?"

"Yes, the celebrated detective who has sworn to capture Arséne Lupin. Ah! I can understand now why we did not receive any news from this side of the Atlantic. Ganimard was here! And he always keeps his business secret."

"Then you think he will arrest Arséne Lupin?"

"Who can tell? The unexpected always happens when Arséne Lupin is concerned in the affair."

"Oh!" she exclaimed, with that morbid curiosity peculiar to women, "I should like to see him arrested."

"You will have to be patient. No doubt Arséne Lupin has already seen his enemy and will not be in a hurry to leave the steamer."

The passengers were now leaving the steamer. Leaning on his umbrella, with an air of careless indifference, Ganimard appeared to be paying no attention to the crowd that was hurrying down the gangway. The Marquis de Raverdan, Major

Rawson, the Italian Rivolta, and many others had already left the vessel when Rozaine appeared. Poor Rozaine!

"Perhaps it is he, after all," said Miss Nelly to me. "What do you think?"

"I think it would be very interesting to have Ganimard and Rozaine in the same picture. You take the camera. I am loaded down."

I gave her the camera, but too late for her to use it. Rozaine was already passing the detective. An American officer, standing behind Ganimard, leaned forward and whispered in his ear. The French detective shrugged his shoulders and Rozaine passed on. Then, my God, who was Arséne Lupin?

"Yes," said Miss Nelly, aloud, "who can it be?"

Not more than twenty people now remained on board. She scrutinized them one by one, fearful that Arséne Lupin was not amongst them.

"We cannot wait much longer," I said to her.

She started toward the gangway. I followed. But we had not taken 10 steps when Ganimard barred our passage.

"Well, what is it?" I exclaimed.

"One moment, monsieur. What's your hurry?"

"I am escorting mademoiselle."

"One moment," he repeated, in a tone of authority. Then, gazing into my eyes, he said: "Arséne Lupin, is it not?"

I laughed, and replied: "No, simply Bernard d'Andrezy."

"Bernard d'Andrezy died in Macedonia three years ago."

"If Bernard d'Andrezy were dead, I should not be here. But you are mistaken. Here are my papers."

"They are his; and I can tell you exactly how they came into your possession."

"You are a fool!" I exclaimed. "Arséne Lupin sailed under the name of R—

"Yes, another of your tricks; a false scent that deceived them at Havre. You play a good game, my boy, but this time luck is against you."

I hesitated a moment. Then he hit me a sharp blow on the right arm, which caused me to utter a cry of pain. He had struck the wound, yet unhealed, referred to in the telegram.

I was obliged to surrender. There was no alternative. I turned to Miss Nelly, who had heard everything. Our eyes met; then she glanced at the Kodak I had placed in her hands, and made a gesture that conveyed to me the impression that she understood everything. Yes, there, between the narrow folds of black leather, in the hollow center of the small object that I had taken the precaution to place in her hands before Ganimard arrested me, it was there I had deposited Rozaine's 20,000 francs and Lady Jerland's pearls and diamonds.

Oh! I pledge my oath that, at that solemn moment, when I was in the grasp of Ganimard and his two assistants, I was perfectly indifferent to everything, to my arrest, the hostility of the people, everything except this one question: What will Miss Nelly do with the things I had confided to her?

In the absence of that material and conclusive proof, I had nothing to fear; but would Miss Nelly decide to furnish that proof? Would she betray me? Would she act the part of an enemy who cannot forgive, or that of a woman whose scorn is softened by feelings of indulgence and involuntary sympathy?

She passed in front of me. I said nothing, but bowed very low. Mingled with the other passengers, she advanced to the gangway with my Kodak in her hand. It occurred to me that she would not dare to expose me publicly, but she might do so when she reached a more private place. However, when she had passed only a few feet down the gangway, with a movement of simulated awkwardness, she let the camera fall into the water between the vessel and the pier. Then she walked down the gangway, and was quickly lost to sight in the crowd. She had passed out of my life forever.

For a moment, I stood motionless. Then, to Ganimard's great astonishment, I muttered: "What a pity that I am not an honest man!"

Such was the story of his arrest as narrated to me by Arsène Lupin himself. The various incidents, which I shall record in writing at a later day, have established between us certain ties, shall I say of friendship? Yes, I venture to believe that Arsène Lupin honors me with his friendship, and it is through friendship that he occasionally calls on me, and brings, into the silence of my library, his youthful exuberance of spirits, the contagion of his enthusiasm, and the mirth of a man for whom destiny has naught but favors and smiles.

His portrait? How can I describe him? I have seen him twenty times and each time he was a different person; even he himself said to me on one occasion: "I no longer know who I am. I cannot recognize myself in the mirror." Certainly, he was a great actor, and possessed a marvelous faculty for disguising himself. Without the slightest effort, he could adopt the voice, gestures and mannerisms of another person.

"Why," said he, "why should I retain a definite form and feature? Why not avoid the danger of a personality that is ever the same? My actions will serve to identify me."

Then he added, with a touch of pride: "So much the better if no one can ever say with absolute certainty: There is Arséne Lupin! The essential point is that the public may be able to refer to my work and say, without fear of mistake: Arséne Lupin did that!"

Glossary

abhorrent—strongly opposed

abstainer—one who deliberately and often with an effort of self-denial refrains from an action or practice

affable—courteous, sociable

akin—essentially similar, related, or compatible

alighted—to come down from something (such as a vehicle)

allayed—to subdue; reduce in intensity or severity

aquiline—curving like an eagle's beak

assent—to agree to something, especially after thoughtful consideration

audacity—bold or arrogant disregard of normal restraints

auricula—a spring flower, a species of Primula, or primrose

auspicious—something favorable

ballads—a simple song; a slow romantic or sentimental song

Bedlam—popular name for insane asylum in London

bereaved—suffering the death of a loved one

bethought—to cause oneself to be reminded

blackguard (pronounced blaggard)—a thoroughly unprincipled person, a scoundrel; a foul-mouthed person

brooding—to think anxiously or gloomily about something; being depressed

burnished—made shiny by rubbing or polishing an object

calyx—the usually green outer whorl of a flower consisting of sepals

capacious—containing a great deal; spacious

careworn—showing the effect of grief or anxiety

charwoman—a cleaning woman, especially in a large building

chateau (plural: chateaux)—a French castle; French manor house; a large country house

Chaucer—English poet, 1342–1400

circumlocution—indirect, talking around something; the use of too many words

"City"—refers to the financial district of London

cogwheels—a wheel with a tooth on the rim; a gear

coleopterist—one who studies beetles and weevils

colloquy—discussion; conversation

condescended—to have behaved in such a way that shows others that you think you are superior to them

contritely—grieving and penitent for a sin or shortcoming

conversant—having knowledge or experience with

corpulent—very fat

countenance—a calm expression

courtier—noblemen and women at the court of a king or queen

criminologist—one who makes a scientific study of crime, or criminals, and of penal treatment

cudgel—a short heavy club

dado—a decorative molding on the lower portion of an interior wall

dandy—a man who gives exaggerated attention to personal appearance

dastardly—characterized by underhandedness or treachery

dejection—depression

despoiled—stripped; robbed; ruined

dilettante—a dabbler in an art or a field of knowledge; an amateur

disconcerted—thrown into confusion

disconsolate—cheerless; dejected; downcast

disheartening—causing to lose one's spirit or morale

dissipation—squandered in pursuit of pleasure such as keeping late hours, riotous living, etc.

dodges—sleight-of-hand tricks

dog cart—a light two-wheeled carriage with two seats back-to-back drawn by a horse

droning—a murmuring, humming, or buzzing sound

elicited—to call forth or draw out

eloquent—vividly or movingly expressive or revealing

elytra—hardened forewings of a beetle protecting the thin, membranous hind wings used in flight

emanate—to come from a source

eminent—standing out or above others in some quality or position

emphatically—expressing oneself in forceful speech

enigma—mystery, riddle, or puzzle

entomologist—one who studies insects

entourage—one's attendants or associates

equanimity—evenness of mind when under stress; composure

errant—straying outside the proper path

estimable—valuable

expositor—one who explains

expound—to explain by setting forth in careful and elaborate detail

Faust—the name of a scholar who in legend sells his soul to the devil in exchange for power and knowledge

ferreted—to force out of hiding

flabbergasted—to be overwhelmed with shock, surprise, or wonder

fuming—to be in a state of excited irritation or anger

gasconade—bravado; boasting
geniality—displaying sympathy or friendliness
Golconda—a region in India, famous for its diamonds
grudgingly—unwillingly; reluctant; resentfully

haughtily—blatantly and disdainfully proud
heathen—an uncivilized or irreligious person
heraldic monsters—statues of animals from family crests
huddled—to arrange carelessly or hurriedly; to crowd
    together

idlers—not occupied or employed
imminent—ready to take place
impaled—pierced with something pointed
implacable—not capable of being appeased or changed
incubus—an evil spirit that lies on persons in their sleep
indelible—cannot be removed, washed away, or erased
ineffable—unspeakable
infinitesimal—immeasurably small
ingenuous—innocent
inimitable—incapable of being imitated; equal to none
insular—having a narrow viewpoint
intonation—the rise and fall in pitch of the voice in speech
justified—to prove or show to be just, right, or reasonable
Kodak—early camera manufactured by the Kodak company
kraken—a fabulous Scandinavian sea monster

laden—carrying a load or burden
languid—sluggish; slow

latterly—of late; recently

lodger—roomer

lurid—gruesome; shocking

malevolent—malicious

marshaled—to bring together and order in an appropriate or effective way

martyr—one who suffers or even dies for a cause

ménage—a family, household, house, or home

mental gelatine—use of photographic term to mean "recorded in one's memory"

narcissus—a group of spring flowers that includes the daffodils

Nihilist—A late 19th century Russian revolutionary group who believed that social and political institutions had to be destroyed to make way for new world order

obscure—dark; vague; ambiguous

obtuse—lacking sharpness or quickness

ominously—foreboding evil

ostentaion—excessive display; showy

palpitation—to beat rapidly and strongly

paramount—superior to all others; supreme

parochial—limited; narrow

peerage—members of the nobility of Britain

personage—a person of rank or distinction

pessimistic—gloomy; expecting bad things to happen

philosophers' stone—an imaginary stone, substance, or chemical preparation believed to have the power of changing baser metals into gold

pinion—a gear with a small number of teeth designed to mesh with a larger wheel or rack

placid—serene; calm

premonitory—giving warning

pretext—a purpose or motive assumed to hide the real intention or state of affairs

profligate—wildly extravagant

prosaic—factual; dull; ordinary

providential—occurring by or as if by divine guidance or intervention

prussic acid—hydrocyanic acid; an aqueous solution of hydrogen cyanide; extremely poisonous

puerile—boyish; childish

pugilist—professional boxer

pulp—a magazine or book printed on cheap paper

quarry—one that is sought or pursued

quavery—to utter sounds in tremulous notes; tremble

Race—used it in Chesterton's story to mean "ethnic group."

ransacked—to search thoroughly; to examine closely and carefully

recapitulation—to repeat the principal points or stages of; summarize

resolute—firm determination; steady

reticent—restrained; reluctant

ruefully—regretful; pitiable

rumination—to go over in the mind repeatedly and slowly; contemplation

salons—the reception room of a large house

sanguine—hopeful; confident

sardonic—scorn, mockery, or derision manifested by verbal or facial expression

savant—one of great learning or genius

scarabei—the group of beetles referred to as "scarabs"

scathing—bitterly severe condemnation

scurvily—contemptible

scuttled—to sink or attempt to sink by making holes through the bottom; destroy

sententious—excessive moralizing

serried—to press together in ranks; to crowd together

Shelley—English poet Percy Bysshe Shelley (1792–1822)

sneer—to smile or laugh with scorn or contempt

sordid—dirty; filthy; wretched, squalid

sovereigns—a British gold coin valued at two pounds eighteen shillings, minted only for use abroad

spud—a narrow spade

stem to stern—throughout, thoroughly

taciturn—disinclined to talk by temperament

tantalus—a stand containing visible decanters of liquor secured by a lock; "tantalized" since one can see the decanters but cannot pour from them because they are locked

teetotaler—someone who never drinks alcohol

tenterhooks—in a state of uneasiness, strain, or suspense

toxicologist—someone dealing with poisons and their affects

ulster—a long, loose overcoat, worn by men and women, originally made of fabric from Ulster, Ireland

unfrequented—not often visited or traveled over

unquestionable—indisputable
uproarious—noisy; extremely funny

vengeance—punishment inflicted in retaliation for an injury or offense; retribution
vestige—a trace, mark, or visible sign left by something vanished or lost
visage—the face, countenance, or appearance of a person

writhing—to twist so as to distort; to suffer keenly

zoology—the branch of biology concerned with classification and properties of animals